FALCON FEATHER

FALCON FEATHER

A STORY OF SALVATION

*Thanks for sharing
Gods promises.*

PAMELA HOFFMAN

Pamela Hoffman 2012

Proverbs 16:9

iUniverse, Inc.
Bloomington

Falcon Feather
A Story of Salvation

This is a work of fiction. All of the characters, names, incidents, organizations, and dialogue in this novel are either the products of the author's imagination or are used fictitiously.

iUniverse books may be ordered through booksellers or by contacting:

iUniverse
1663 Liberty Drive
Bloomington, IN 47403
www.iuniverse.com
1-800-Authors (1-800-288-4677)

ISBN: 978-1-4620-4003-2 (sc)
ISBN: 978-1-4620-4004-9 (hc)
ISBN: 978-1-4620-4005-6 (ebk)

Library of Congress Control Number: 2011919551

Printed in the United States of America

iUniverse rev. date: 12/17/2011

CONTENTS

PROLOGUE

PONDERINGS

I have an internal diary—a book that records the important happenings in my life. Sometimes I write in a journal so I'll remember every detail of an important event, but my brain runs on high all of the time, with all kinds of information zipping rapidly from here to there. I visit with God any time of day; that helps me process things. It's like having a diary; I just don't have to write things down. I think them. I can't write as fast as I think, so this works out well for me. God is always listening and never farther than a breath away. Some people talk to themselves and no one thinks a thing about it. If I ever told anyone that I'm visiting with God when I talk and not just talking to myself, they would laugh at me. But when I stop to think about it, they're the crazy ones. They're visiting with themselves. I, at least, have a divine audience.

CHAPTER 1

CATTAILS, CALAMITY, & CAVES

Red-faced from my escape of the overgrown cattails, I think about last year when I was fourteen and wondering if I'd ever be as tall as the cattails. Well, I'm as tall as those darn exploding fuzz-bombs now. I used to think they looked like big cigars when I was a little boy. Now I'm certain they're the plant's first line of defense. No matter how gently I try to move them out of my way, they explode into an army of little fuzzy seeds that take flight, all of them heading for me like heat-seeking missiles. The fact that I need a haircut isn't to my benefit. I'm going to look like a porcupine with cotton balls all over my head. I hate it when my hair grows out a little and stands straight out in all directions, like a reddish-yellow halo. None of my brothers has coarse, straight hair. Mom calls the color strawberry blond, but I can't honestly think of a single guy who would describe his hair as strawberry blond.

"Achoo! Achoo! Achoo!" Sneezes always come in threes for me.

"Why do you always fish over there in the cattails?" Braden complains from across the pond. "You'll be sneezing all day and scaring off the fish!"

"I'll not be the one to chase the fish away. And for your information, I fish over here because this is where the spring is, *bro*," I call back, exaggerating the word bro to put him in his place. "The big fish like to cool down in that cool, fresh, natural spring water that constantly feeds into the pond. I've already caught five nice ones for supper. You should try it sometime, instead of lying over there, working on your tan."

"Five? We haven't even been here an hour yet. Coda, you're blowin' smoke!" Braden says, eyeing me to see if I'm joking.

I make my way from the west side of the pond to the north. The west side has a slightly steep, rocky wall, with cattails surrounding the southwest, west, and northwest side of the pond. The pond's dam is on the north—earth fills in the gap between my side of the canyon wall and Braden's east side. His is a gentle slope, leveling off with a grassy pasture on the top rim of the canyon. The earthen dam is wide enough to drive a car across.

"Well, I could've had five if I'd wanted," I say with conviction. "I guess the count is closer to one, but he's a big one!"

"I figured as much," Braden says and stretches out.

As I swat at the fuzz balls clinging to my sweaty bare skin, I wish I'd kept my shirt on, but it's so humid in the cattails I'd decided to lose the shirt. I notice how Braden's hair has grown out. His hair lays down when it gets a little length in it. He takes pride in how he looks, even when he's at the pond, fishing. He's clean-shaven, and his short, dark-brown hair is combed. Braden has a tan that gives him a healthy glow. I could stay outside every day and only get more freckles. I don't think I'll ever need to shave, because I have more pimples than whiskers.

What is up with all the pimples, God? You know how important it is for a guy to look his best as he enters high school. Sophomore year is coming up next month! How about You dry up these gross things once and for all? Maybe You could do that for my birthday in November.

"I'm going exploring downstream," I say, planning to follow the path along the northeast side of the dam next to the canyon wall. I run across the top of the dam where we've been fishing, and a cloud of fuzzy cattail puffs that have dislodged from my hair follow me like that dirt cloud of Pig-Pen's from the *Peanuts* cartoon strip. They hover, floating silently on the air, keeping pace with me as I sneeze all the way across the earthen embankment.

Between sneezes I call out, "I'll be back for lunch." I hike to the path leading over the backside. Over the years, the trees and brush have taken root on the dam, leaving only the one path to the bottom.

"Okay. I'll meet you here later. I want to fish," Braden replies, mumbling something under his breath and chuckling.

My older brother, Braden, is the best big brother. He may be four and a half years older than me, but he doesn't make me feel like a little kid. I have three younger brothers—Liam, Eli, and Fuller. Now, they're little kids! My two older sisters, Dulcie and Alexa, between Braden and me, add just enough cushion between us boys to keep the fights down. Sisters are good mediators, but Braden is still my favorite. He takes me fishing and hunting with him and tolerates my energy levels better than anyone else does. I'm hyperactive and very impulsive most of the time.

Our family farm is at the edge of Southard's United States Gypsum property. Dad works for them and does the training of new personnel. I find the history of the gypsum plant fascinating. I'm amazed that in the early years, they would hand dig and mine the gypsum from these canyons. There is also a salt creek just a few miles from here where salt was mined. The canyon's erosion exposes various layers of gypsum rock and red shale. George Southard mined that gypsum from 1905 to 1912. He then sold it to the United States Gypsum Corporation, which is our neighbor to the north and east of our farm. Our farm is rich in many ways, and the history surrounding it is just one of them—nomadic Indian tribes visited the land before the gypsum company. The natural spring here never goes dry, even in the driest seasons, so it would've been a good source of water for the Indians. Looking at the layers on the canyon wall, I think of the jawbreaker in my pocket. I pop it into my mouth and stroll along.

God, You put the earth together like one huge jawbreaker, didn't You? You wrapped layers of minerals and layers of rocks for us to find. What else have You hidden for me today?

My imagination runs wild as I make my way down the back of the pond's dam. I have a vivid imagination, and I can almost see the Indians of long ago, hunting deer nearby. I gaze at my surroundings as if I'm watching a live theater production. We've found several arrowheads over the years around the spring. I wonder if I'll find any in the creek bottom today. My thoughts return to my own private outdoor theater. The Indians are dressed in buckskins, riding uniquely spotted paint ponies of chocolate, licorice, and cream. The ponies' colorful patches give definition to their muscles as they trot along. The buffalo, deer, and rabbits are in abundance, along with the grass and fresh water from the spring. My colorful imaginings help me to see the perfect place for a teepee encampment on the flat top of the canyon's eastern wall. I imagine the young boys and girls helping the women as they set up their camp of teepees. All the adolescent boys and men would be getting their bows and arrows ready for the hunt. Their hunt tomorrow would be successful, because I'm sure there'll be deer just around this narrowing of the canyon.

I walk barefoot on native grass that is soggy from the water continually flowing from the overflow pipe in the dam. This allows the creek to have a constant flow of fresh water for the animals downstream. I turn the corner, and the canyon broadens, revealing a large area that's deep in the center and shallow along the edges. I duck, pretending an arrow has whizzed by my shoulder. I turn my head to see what my imaginary Indian companion is shooting at, and I see a real rabbit. After chasing the rabbit downstream, I see that this part of the ravine widens out and is thick with trees and brush near the canyon's walls. I must've run about fifteen yards from the dam. I stand now in knee-deep water and notice that it isn't moving much; in fact, it's pooling. I'm very observant that way. Mom says I am visually distracted by things.

God, I think You gave me a heightened awareness of Your world. The reason I jump from one thing to another isn't because I have ADD; it's because You also gave me an urgency to experience everything You've made.

I look around, wondering why the water has stopped flowing. The pool gets increasingly deeper for the next twenty-five yards, so I move to a ledge above the water level, and I find the answer. A beaver has set up residence on the creek. I look around and, not seeing the rodent, I confidently give him fair warning, calling out in a commanding voice, "Grandma says you're going to have to go, Mr. Beaver. You tried this a few years ago, and Grandma took care of you. Well, Grandma's not here, but Coda, defender of the burr oaks, is here!" I beat my bare chest for good measure and stand tall in my cut-off jean shorts. A few fuzz balls dislodge from my bare skin, though others remain in my hair as I look at my reflection in the still water.

Hearing no response, I move closer and think that the beaver's amazing engineering talents must definitely be God-given. By the size of the dam and lodge, I guess there are probably at least two beavers living here. Beavers mate for life, and so up to two litters could be living with their parents, based on the size of the beaver lodge.

I say loudly, "Mr. and Mrs. Beaver, I hope you don't think that you are like a cousin or anything to me, just because you have a dad, mom, and kids. You beavers have killed the burr oaks!" They've chewed all the way around the tree trunks. Grandma told me the summer before she died that one day, the burr oaks would be completely wiped out of this area. Even now, the burr oaks are nearly all gone. "Sorry, Mr. Beaver," I call out, "but you're going to have to move." Dad has said if the beaver pond backs up to the bottom of my pond's dam, it'll weaken it, causing my dam to give way, and that's another reason Grandma sent the beavers packing. I raise my voice one more time, shouting, "You're not going to wreck my dam!" I walk next to the canyon wall and come to the beaver's dam. It stretches from one side of the canyon's wall to the other, making a fairly wide pond. I read a book on beavers when I was little and remember that it takes a half-mile of habitat to support one family. I try to stand on the shale edge of the pond and pull the limbs from the dam. The sheer cliff wall behind me makes it difficult to bend over. I have to be careful not to land headfirst in the water.

Don't laugh, God. I know You have a sense of humor. I dare You to try it—stand with Your back to a wall and then bend over and pick up something from the floor . . . or a cloud . . . in front of You. See? I told You. I imagine God is laughing.

I look around but don't see the beavers. I wade in about chest high and begin tearing the logs, limb by limb, from the dam. The water begins to flow over the top, slowly at first, and then it picks up speed. That is when it happens.

Pow! Pow! Pow!

Vibrations ripple across the water where the bullets must've hit. I whirl around, searching the canyon walls for the hunter, but I remember that July is not hunting season. Is someone shooting at me? I don't think imaginary Indians can come to life.

"Braden! Did you hear that?" I scream. And then thinking that I sound like a girl, I shout again, lowering my voice this time, "Braden!"

Oo! Oo! Oo! A mournful seal-like barking is right behind me. Is that an Indian calling to his buddy? Am I surrounded? Spinning in the now waist-deep water, I spot him. He's large; he's brown with slick, dark hair and beady eyes, black as coal, glaring at me. The top of his head and his eyes are all that's above the water. Volumes are spoken in those few seconds between me and Mr. Beaver. I can almost hear him say, "How dare you destroy my home? The missus and I just finished the remodeling." He'd speak in beaver language, of course—a language in which I am fluent, by the way.

The "gunshots" now made sense—it was the beaver, slapping his powerful flat tail on the water, sounding the alarm for the other beavers. *Other beavers!* I look left, right, and behind me as I back toward the canyon wall and the path leading back to Braden. Mr. Beaver moves closer. He swims effortlessly. I, on the other hand, can't seem to move where I want to go. The current is pulling me.

"Beaver! Braden, a beaver is after me! Help me!" I scream.

The hair on the back of my neck stands up, and I feel like there is something or someone right behind me. Goose bumps begin to pop up on my skin. The expression "My hair stood up on end" is literally true. As the hair stands up, it pulls the skin slightly, making goose bumps. I try to climb out of the water, but I seem to panic a little as I feel pokes and scratches on my legs and feet. I mean, it could be the claws of a mega-beaver or a bunch of baby beavers! I look back . . . and the beaver is submerged. He's under the water, sneaking up on me. I know he is!

"Help me!" I sound like a girl again, and I don't even care.

The logs I'd dislodged let the water begin to spill over the top of the dam, and it's moving more limbs. My long, boney legs get tangled in the debris underwater, and I go under. Spitting and sputtering, I resurface and find I'm floating with the current of rushing water, closer to the dam and the family's lodge home.

"Oh no!" I scream.

It's the last place I want to be, so I grab a branch that's hanging over the water's edge. It's too small to hold my weight and breaks, sending me into the water again. Squealing, I realize the water is not over my head; I can stand up at any time. Gee whiz, I've got to get a grip on myself and get out of here. The logs roll and spin, flipping me flat on my back for a third time. Lying on the bottom of the now-drained pond, I tilt my head backwards and peer over the top of my forehead. The scene is upside down, but I see not one but two large, smiling beavers lumbering toward me.

"Braden!" I scream again.

They look happy—no, angry! Those big orange tusk-like teeth are not smiling; they are ready to chew me up and spit me out! I'm done for; I know it! I manage to get upright one more time. Most of the water is going down the creek bed, leaving the pond looking kind of small now. I glance over my shoulder, and the beavers are halfway across the dry pond, still coming toward me. My only chance of survival is to leap out of the water and onto the shale shelf, just above where the pond used to be. I make it and turn to see one beaver lumbering up the side of the damp pond; the other is blocking my getaway, should I try to go downhill. Mr. Beaver takes his time in toying with me, like a cat would do with a mouse—trapping it and then letting it go, only to trap it again. I can't use the path in either direction. Downstream is Mrs. Beaver, and upstream are thickets of thorny foliage. Mr. Beaver continues toward me. The only way to save myself is to climb the wall. I move closer and find a couple of rocks to hold on to and a couple of rocks to step upon. Slowly, I climb higher and higher. I'm about three feet off of the ground when I feel his whiskers brush the calf of my leg.

Someone not as familiar with the wild as I am might think it was only the leaves of the bush, but the outdoorsman that I am, I know the difference. I'm so sure it's a beaver. I can see in my mind those enormous orange tusk-like teeth biting down on the soft tissue of the back of my leg. Up, up I climb! Nothing like an image like that to get a person motivated. When I'm about six feet off the ground, the rocks I'm using as handholds give way—and down I come, screaming like a girl again. I'll be glad when my voice decides to land an octave lower. Before I hit the ground, my fall is broken by the two-inch thorns of the thicket, which first become entangled in my cut-off jean shorts and then hold me off of the ground by grabbing me and thrusting deeply into my skin. I'm hanging upside down by my pants and skin. I'm wedged between the wall of the canyon and a bunch of thorny bushes! At least my face is toward the cliff wall and not toward the thorns, even if I did scrape it in a place or two. It's important to always find the positive in life. I try to free myself, but I'm stuck tight, and with each movement, the thorns rip my flesh. I wonder if my long toes look like tender burr oak limbs to a beaver. Why do I think of such horrors?

"Help me, Braden! Help!" I scream as loudly as I can.

And I hear Braden mocking me. *"Help me, Braden! Help!"*

How dare he make fun! I call again, "Braden, I'm serious!"

"Braden, I'm serious!"

What in the world is going on? That's not like him. Then I have an idea, so I test my theory. "Hello!"

"Hello!"

Just as I thought: it's an echo, and it's coming from the wall. I see a crack running through the layer of rock and an opening at the bottom of the wall. There must be a cave. How exciting! I can't wait to tell Braden. I feel cool air on my face, and the air continues to move over my face like a steady breeze. This is definitely a cave, and one with another opening somewhere, by the feel of this draft of air.

"Coda, how in blazes did you get back there?" Braden asks. He begins to pick at and pull the thorns bushes back so he can reach me.

"Braden, I found a cave, I think," I say with excitement.

"Coda, you have been screaming bloody murder, like you were being mauled by bears or something. I nearly broke my neck, running down here just to see a cave—not even a cave; it's a crack in the wall!" Braden pokes himself with a thorn while pulling one out of me. He seems mad, so I decide I'd better tell the whole story. The sweat on his athletic body shows the exertion from his run down the dam and through the humidity of the canyon. His damp face scowls, and his hazel eyes snap from the green of the leaves to the blue of the sky.

"There was a beaver after me, and I fell in here when I tried to climb up the wall," I explain. "Watch your back, Braden. That beaver is stealth-like. There're two of them, but the male is the one after me. They may look slow, but they can put on a move when they want. I'm sure some of these scratches are from his huge claws. You should see his teeth! Look around to see if he's gone, because if he isn't, you might not fare as well as I have. Find something to protect yourself."

"The only thing I see is a skinny little brother hanging upside down, tangled up in a thorn bush, wedged next to a rock face wall. You don't look like you're faring very well yourself. What did you do to the beaver anyway?" Braden asks as he looks around. Then he tries to free me, while not slicing himself in the process. Poking himself, he yells, "Ouch!"

"I was tearing down his dam so he'd move. Grandma said they love to eat burr oaks and that we don't have many left, that those trees are almost extinct," I say, hearing my echo.

"Those trees are almost extinct."

"Do you hear that echo?" I ask. "I bet there's a big cave. We should explore it. I feel a cool breeze coming out of this crack. There must be another opening somewhere for the air to draw through here. Wasn't it lucky of me to fall right here, with my face smashed up to the wall? Just think—I might've missed discovering this cave if this hadn't happened." I prattle on, realizing that when my attention goes skittering across time like this, it makes me sound unfocused.

"Ouch!" Braden yells again when my twisting to see the cave causes him to get poked. "Coda, stay still and tell me about the beaver!" Braden shouts. He is more than a little upset with those thorns, I'm sure. They're a pain.

"He's big, furry, and mean," I respond.

"I'm going up to the pickup to get a hatchet and a shovel," Braden says angrily.

"That's a good idea. Get that big one with the hatchet first. Then what? Are you going to bury him with the shovel?" I ask, realizing as I finish my thought that it doesn't make much sense and that Braden always makes sense. Braden doesn't answer. "Don't leave me. Where's that beaver? Look for that beaver first. Do you see him?" I plead, totally serious this time. I try to turn my head to look at the canyon and end up poking my face with thorns. My only view is of this crack in the wall.

"You stay right there," Braden laughs. I can't believe he's laughing! "I'll be back. This is the first time all day that I'll know for sure where to find you and that you won't be getting into trouble while I'm gone. I may get a little fishing in after all." He continues to cackle as he walks up the dam ever so slowly.

"Braden, don't joke! Where's the beaver?" I exclaim. "It's not nice to torment a guy when he's down! I mean up . . . or upside down! Oh! You know what I mean!"

"It may take me an hour or two to find that hatchet and shovel," he calls from the path leading to the dam.

CHAPTER 2

SOAKING & SINKING IN SODA

I'm up to my neck in a bathtub of baking soda and water, with Eli adding yet another box.

I'm submerged to my shoulders, and Eli is dusting baking soda over my ears and neck. I state the obvious. "Eli, I don't need any baking soda on my head!"

"Okay," Eli says and pours the rest on my shoulders. I have to totally submerge in the water to get all the soda rinsed off again.

Mom has gone to town to get more butterfly bandages. It's a staple of our house, with so many boys.

"Braden, can we go to the pond tomorrow?" I beg as he brushes his teeth.

"No," Braden says, with a mouth full of foamy toothpaste.

"Please? I'll do your chores tomorrow if you will take me to the pond," I say, trying to bribe him.

He spits his toothpaste out in the sink and says, "Coda, I've got to work out tomorrow because I skipped today to go fishing with you. No, I can't take you."

"You could carry me all the way to the pond. That would be better than lifting weights," I offer.

Braden is gargling. He looks at me and then spits the mouthwash out in the tub. Eli chuckles; I glare at Braden and say nothing. I want to go to the pond and explore the cave, so I don't want him mad at me.

"I said no! I'm in enough trouble. Now shut up!" Braden exclaims.

"Dad is home. I hear his truck," I announce, thinking I'll work on Braden later.

Braden leaves the bathroom, and Eli follows, closing the door, but I can hear Dad and Braden talking in the living room.

"I told you to watch out for the others if you take them to the pond. What were you thinking, letting him dig around in a beaver's dam?" Dad sounds off. "Where were you, and why was he alone?"

"Dad, it was an accident. I didn't know he was going to dig in a beaver's dam. I didn't even know there was a beaver's dam," Braden explains. "He was only out of sight maybe twenty minutes, and I could hear him talking to himself all the time. Dad, I'm sorry. I really am." Braden sounds like he feels awful.

If I'm honest with myself, I know that I'm the one responsible for my actions. I'll be sixteen in four months. I should be able to make better decisions. I know in the past my ADD has kept me distracted, and my hyperactivity makes me a little too impulsive for my own good. But dang it, everyone should be able to count on me.

I lean over the edge of the tub to get closer to the closed bathroom door and call out, "Dad, it isn't Braden's fault. I ran off!"

"We'll finish this later," Dad says to Braden. He opens the bathroom door and starts to smile but catches himself when he sees me. "How are you feeling?" Dad asks. He grabs a towel and pretends to wipe his already dry face. He keeps his mouth covered for a moment, but his eyes twinkle and as he clears his throat, it almost sounds like suppressed laughter. Braden walks over to the sink and puts away the toothpaste.

"I'll be fine, Dad. It wasn't Braden's fault," I state. "Just think, Dad—if I hadn't fallen, I would've never found the cave!"

"Cave? There's more to the story than beavers?" Dad asks, looking at both of us and dropping the towel. I must've been wrong about the laughter, because there isn't a trace of laughter now.

I nod. "It's about twenty-five yards from the dam. Can I show you tomorrow if you get home before dark? Please, Dad?" I ask hopefully.

"All right. I'll try to get home early, but you stay away from there until I see what you've found." Dad makes eye contact with me, and I swear I saw a chink in that hardened face. His eyes twinkle and then he whirls around to face Braden. "Braden, make sure of it!" Dad says. Although his back is to me, I swear I hear a chuckle in his voice. Then he strides toward the kitchen, where I hear the muffled voices of Mom and Dad. Then there's laughter. I guess Mom is telling him a joke.

The next morning, I'm ready to go to the cave. I have flashlights, matches, candles, water, and Tylenol. I hurt all over, but I wouldn't miss checking out the cave for anything. It's like the cave is a magnet, and I'm the only piece of metal around. It's drawing me to it with a powerful force. Mom comes into my room and sees my supplies. The clock reads 10:00 a.m.

"Coda, I want you to lie down and just close your eyes," Mom says. "It's time for more Tylenol, and maybe you can rest. It'll be hours before your dad is home."

"Okay, but if I fall asleep and Dad comes home, wake me," I answer. "I didn't sleep much last night. I couldn't seem to find a comfortable position. I felt like old Dancer, pacing round and round his dog blanket before lying down. I tried lying on my back, front, sides, every which-a-way, but everywhere hurt."

Mom has a glass of water and the Tylenol in her hands. She hands them to me, straightens the covers on my bed, and fluffs my pillow as she says, "I promise to wake you the minute I hear the truck."

I doze off, and when I awaken, the sun is going down. I watch TV until Dad comes home. He's late, as usual. I meet him at the door with my hands on my boney hips, and I try to furrow my eyebrows with disappointment. A person can't be expected to put on a really convincing frown with butterfly bandages pulling his face into a pleasant expression. I bet the Joker on *Batman* felt like this when his face was frozen into a smile.

"I'll try to get home earlier tomorrow," Dad promises. Smiling at Mom, he says, "He looks like a road map, with those bandages crisscrossing his face and arms. See?" He points to a spot on my arm and laughs. "Here's a road and an intersection with a railroad track."

"You don't have to laugh about it!" I exclaim indignantly and march off to my room.

It's like that for a week, and finally, on Sunday, Dad is off work. He never works on Sunday; we go to church as a family. Dad went to seminary to be a Baptist preacher, like his dad and granddad, but the Holy Spirit led him in a different direction. He felt he could witness to men at a job. So he witnesses daily to all he meets, and then on Sundays, he likes to take a nap in the afternoon, but instead of napping, today he takes the whole family to the pond. We chop the remaining thorn bushes from the opening of the cave. Dad digs away the crumbly rock, making the opening about three feet high and wide. He shines his flashlight inside. I start to crawl in, but he yanks me back, which pulls some of the butterfly bandages loose and makes the cuts bleed again.

"Don't you ever go inside a cave, crevice, or hole in these canyons! There could be rattlesnakes!" he barks at me, but then he turns to all of us. "I don't want any of you ever crawling, walking, or hiding in any place that looks like this. We'll do our exploring in the dead of winter, when we're sure the snakes are hibernating. 'We' means that your mother or I must be with you. This cave is off limits. No one is allowed downstream any longer."

After cooking hot dogs and roasting marshmallows, we go home. I try to keep my mind off the cave, but I can't. I don't think I can wait until winter.

Please, Lord, make the cave safe somehow, and let me be the first to explore it. Amen.

CHAPTER 3

OVERPOWERED, OVERWHELMED, & OBSESSED

I am totally consumed with the thought of exploring the cave. I approach the subject again at the dinner table. I spit it out as if I'm going to burst, "Next month is my birthday, and I know just what I want."

Dad is taking a bite of food, so Mom asks, smiling, "What do you want, Coda?"

"I want to go to the cave and explore it. You said wait until it cooled off. It hit freezing last night," I announce.

"Coda, when you last asked me, for the umpteenth time, when we could go, I told you if you brought up the subject of the cave again, I wouldn't let you go at all," Dad reminds me threateningly.

"I thought you just meant if I brought it up before it was time to go. You said after it cooled down, and it cooled down last night," I say. I know I sound petulant, but I'm not; I'm just stating facts.

"Coda, it was also seventy degrees the day before yesterday. We've not had enough days of cold weather yet. You're too obsessed with that cave. We can't even have a discussion at the dinner table without you bringing up some fact about stalactites or stalagmites," Dad complains.

Fuller loves geology and always talks with me at the table about the topic, but today he says, "Yeah, even I'm getting tired of your constant talk about the cave."

Mom furrows her eyebrows, like she does when she's worried. "I'm concerned about you," she says, "because you seem to be so infatuated with this cave. I just don't understand why you can't let it go."

"Never mind. Forget I said anything. Get me whatever you want or nothing at all. May I be excused from the table? I have a test tomorrow," I say, standing up. I add, "Supper was delicious. Thanks, girls and Mom." I immediately feel awful about my outburst. That's not like me to be so all-consumed about something. Ever since finding the cave it has taken control over my life. I know what it's like to not be able to control my impulsive behavior, but this is different. It is frightening how strong my need to go inside the cave has become.

I go straight to my bedroom, close the door, and get out my algebra. It isn't long before I'm joined by Eli and Fuller. They know better than to speak to me when I'm this hot over something. They each grab a book and lie down on their beds to read. Braden must be helping to clear the table, I figure, and he probably did my chore of carrying out the trash. I'd forgotten all about it being my turn. *Oh well,* I think, *I'll thank him later.*

"Coda, can I come in?" Braden asks at the door. It isn't necessary for any of us to ask permission—boys share a room, and the girls share a room—so it seems odd that he asked.

"Sure, it's your room too," I answer. I wish I had a room of my own, as we all have, at one time or another.

"I talked to Dad, and we can go to the pond over fall break. I told him how we're planning to add to the fish supply for winter," Braden said as he went straight to his bunk.

"What did he say?" I asked, keeping my eyes glued to the algebra page. I didn't want anyone to see the hope that leapt within me.

"He said yes, as long as *you* stayed away from the cave. He wants to be there when we go in the first time," Braden says, staring at me. I guess he wants to see how I'll react.

"That'll be great. Shall we leave this Thursday? It's the first day of fall break. I'm sure he wants to be the first to go inside. He found the spring and the first arrowheads. It only makes sense that he would want to see the cave first. It's his land," I say, with more understanding than I feel. On one hand, I know my dad is protecting me, but on the other hand, I'm jealous. I don't know where all of these negative emotions are coming from when I'm told I can't go inside the cave. I'm not usually upset when I'm told no.

It's almost like there is another person living inside of me, commanding my actions.

"Okay, we'll leave early, before sunup, and fill the freezer," Braden answers. Smiling, he begins to read his literature. He's hoping for a scholarship this year in some field of journalism or sports. He reads every spare minute he has after football practice.

On Thursday morning, I pull on Braden's arm, almost dragging him out of his bed and onto the floor. "Braden, come on! It's time to go. We've gotta beat the sunrise."

"Okay, buddy," Braden says. "I'm up. Let me grab something to drink."

He gets out of bed and heads to the kitchen for the coffee, which is already made. He grabs a cup and then goes back to our room to get dressed. I pour the rest of the coffee into a thermos. It's the last thing to load. I bring along a Mountain Dew. I may need lots of energy today. I'd already loaded the tackle box, rods and reels, sack of food, and backpack with miscellaneous things like bandages and twelve fish stringers. I plan on kidding Braden about catching over a hundred fish. Thinking about how busy we'll be today, I grab the six-pack of Mountain Dew.

"You're not bringing books, are you?" I complain when Braden shows up with his literature book.

"Yes, I am. I have to get some reading done for my literature teacher. She's helped keep me on track for applying for a scholarship. It would be great if I got it, but if that doesn't work, I have Coach working on some scholarships to the local colleges," Braden says, putting an end to that fight. How can a guy fight with a senior who's college bound? Braden acts more like an adult every day—gross.

"Okay, but we get to fish sometime today," I state. I can't be expected to carry the whole load of fishing. I'm disappointed, because I'd planned on Braden's doing the biggest share of the fishing so I could slip off and explore a little. *Well, let me think about this a minute. Braden gets totally absorbed in his reading and doesn't notice anything going on around him.* This might work out better than I thought.

I ask, "What's the big deal about moving away to college?" I'm going to miss Braden, but I don't dare tell him. That would just be too lame.

"I can't wait to be out on my own, alone. I don't know what alone feels like. All I can remember is always sharing a room—first with the girls when we were little and later with you guys. Don't get me wrong; I love all of you, but imagine—no snoring but your own," Braden says, smiling. He knows he's the only one who snores. He says we do too sometimes, but I don't believe him.

"I guess that would be cool," I say, sadly reflecting on what life might be like next fall.

Mom enters the room with her keys and two jackets. She throws the jackets in our direction. It's understood that she wants us to wear them. "Let's go, boys," she says. "I've got a ton of bakery deliveries today. If I'm going to get them finished in time to make it back to the pond by dark, we have to scoot." Mom breezes by us and then out the door into the twilight of early morning.

The leaves are changing color, and as we wind through the pond pasture, the pickup's headlights reflect the color of the leaves back to us. A railroad track splits the back pasture with the spring-fed pond pasture. We stop to open a couple of gates on each side of the tracks. We leave them open so Mom will only have to close them on her way back. We didn't see any cattle in this part of the pasture, so surely they won't get out. Mom rolls to a stop at the top of the west side of the pond, and we all can't take our eyes off of the amazing sunrise. A few clouds reflect the sun's distant glow of purples and reds. The sun has yet to peek above the horizon. The air is crisp and sweet-smelling, like a fresh rain shower. We bail out of the pickup, grab our things, and thank Mom for the lift. We could've walked, but it's a long way on foot. I dump the tackle box, food, and backpack at the top of the dam, and then I head for the cattails and the spring. I'm thankful for my jacket—it's pretty chilly, which makes me smile. That means cold again last night and cooler days, so there shouldn't be any snakes out and about.

"Coda, put that stuff on the picnic table. The ants will have more of our lunch than we will if you leave it on the ground," Braden says. He picks up the tackle box and heads on around the pond to where the diving board once stood. It's shaded in the morning, and he can bake in the sun in the afternoon. He likes to soak up the heat, because he's more cold-blooded than I am. I throw the sack of food on the table and take off again.

I ask, "Do you want six of these stringers?" I'm grinning, holding all twelve of them.

"I think we can just leave them with the tackle box," Braden says. "You take one, and I'll have one. If we get them full of fish, we'll know where to find the extra stringers. Besides, we may need a break by then."

Grabbing one, I shoot him a grin and say, "Bet I catch the most, sucker!"

"We'll see, Stinky!" Braden exclaims.

I run to the spring. I cast out to the clear, deep cavity that the spring has made and then plant my rod's handle deep into the mud. I begin to whack away at the cattails, making a small area like a tiny room. I turn, and my bobber is under the water. I have a fish!

"I got one, Braden! I got one!" I call out as I reel the fish to the bank. It's a nice-sized bass.

"Yeah, sure you do!" Braden says sarcastically. I know he doesn't believe me.

I put the fish on my stringer and put it back in the water. I bait my hook again and cast it in the pool of cool water, propping my pole up again. Then I grab the stringer and head straight up the steep hill on my side of the pond. As soon as I clear the six-foot-tall cattails, I hold up my fish. Out of a cloud of cattail fuzz-bombs, my fish and I emerge. "Hey, bro, check this one out!" I say, all smug and triumphant. "*Achoo! Achoo! Achoo!*"

"Great. We'll catch our goal before Mom gets back. Good job, Stinky!" Braden calls back.

Stinky. He knows I hate that nickname. The kids used to call me that when I was little because everything gave me gas. What did they think a two-year-old would do? Discreetly excuse himself and go to the bathroom?

I bark back, "Game on, fool! I'll fill my stringer before you fill yours."

I bound back and get my fish back in the water before it dies. Keeping fish alive until we get home to clean them is very important. I look for my bobber—it's gone. I've caught another one! I'm not going to let Braden know this time. I'll just bring a stringer full of fish over to his side of the pond in a little bit.

Two hours pass, and I have a full stringer. Two of the fish are just medium-sized, but that's big enough to keep. To reward myself, I'm going to check out the cave. I march over to the middle of the pond, where a steel post is driven deep in the ground. I fasten my stringer onto it and call out to Braden, "Okay, my stringer's full, and I'm ready for that break. Where's yours?"

"Good job!" Braden responds. "I only have four fish, and they're all medium ones. You've got some really nice ones, Stinky." Braden adds that last word just to get me going.

"I'm going to explore downstream," I say and take off across the top of the dam.

"Coda, don't you dare!" Braden answers. "You know we are not to go exploring without Dad! I'm here to relax, not chase after you all day!"

"I'll only be a minute," I say, disappearing over the edge of the top of the dam.

"Dang it!" Braden says.

He'll have to reel his rod in and stake his fish, so I've got a few minutes. I think about Dad finding the spring and the first arrowheads when he was young. I think to myself, *I'm going to follow in his footsteps. Sorry, Dad. I'm going to be the first one to see the cave.* I know he'll understand, because he's proud of his own discoveries. I wonder what I'll find. Everyone says there won't be stalactites, that it'll be more like Alabaster Caverns—large caverns formed by water washing through, taking the loose sediments with it. Well, those caverns were found by accident, and now they're part of a state park. We've gone to the caverns every year since I was six. When I was little, the three-quarter-mile hike, down and up, out of the cavern seemed extremely long. I was always amazed at the huge chunks of alabaster. They were a part of the ceiling, and boulders had dropped to the floor below as the dirt below them was washed away. Last year, the family took the Lantern Tour, and we saw the caverns as they would've been explored by the first to see them—with only a lantern and no electricity. It was at dusk, and the bats were flying around. The guides told us about the legends surrounding the caverns.

I bet I'll discover a cavern, and we'll become rich, giving tours. Dad will be so proud of me that he'll forget all about grounding me. The cavern I discover might become a state park too! I wonder how to go about applying to be a state park. At the mouth of the cave, I flip on my flashlight, drop to my knees, and begin crawling. I've only a few minutes before Braden comes after me, hauling me out feet first, I'm sure. In my rush to see all that I can, I'm quite a distance inside when it happens. Crawling quickly, I see that there's been a tunnel washed into the side of the hill. It isn't very big—about four, almost five feet across. Not quite enough room to stand. And then I see it—a beautiful striped feather. There aren't any other feathers. There are no bones, as there would be if something had caught the bird and ate it here.

I pick it up and a shudder comes over me. I flash the light around for signs that some carnivorous animal lives nearby, but I see no signs of anything having been here. While my mind wanders to creatures of the deep, the cave opens up, and I can stand. I shine my flashlight straight up, and I can see I'm in a cavern. The wall opposite me is fifty or sixty feet away. I wonder what we'll name my cavern. My flashlight is just a little bigger than a penlight and doesn't have much power, but I can make out some shapes on the opposite wall. One looks like a thick rope ladder, with branches for the rungs woven into it. I can't quite see it, so I decide to move closer. My light is trained on the ladder, and as I take one step forward, my world gives way. I fall, feet first. I hear a crack when my foot hits a rock and pivots sharply. At the same time, I ram my elbow into a rock that was sticking out of the wall. I hear blood-curdling screams that echo off of the walls. I'm in blinding pain, but know the screams must've come from me. The rock has dislocated or broken my shoulder. I'm dizzy, and as I land with a thud, the lights go out—literally and completely.

I awaken in the hospital from crazy dreams. In the dreams, there are falcons, feathers, ladders, caves, and unseen animals with just their teeth showing in the darkness. Blood . . . bones sticking out of flesh . . . my flesh. Then I see a light. I see Braden. He's talking but not making sense. He wants to catch me like a fish and put me on a stringer. There's fire. I feel the bits of ash fall on me. There's an overwhelming sense of danger and something threatening my life—small crackling noises at first and then it's deafening. It's rattlesnakes, rattling all around me. The noise is huge, so the snakes must be huge. I have to listen to Braden—he knows what to do—but I can't hear him over the rattling. He always knows what to do. I do what he tells me, and he reels me in like a fish. I see the light again. I'm falling backwards. Then there's pain and nothingness.

I awaken again from similar crazy dreams. Some things are always the same—the cave, feathers, falcons, ladders, my urgency to get to the ladder. If I could just get to the ladder! Then the dreams change, and there's danger all around, darkness, pain, rattling of snakes, and more pain. Every time I try to make sense of it, a nurse comes in and injects medicine into my IV. Sleep—blissful sleep—always follows the nurses. They have haloes. Maybe I'm in heaven, but I remember the blood, exposed bones, pain, fear, and rattling, and think I must be in hell.

Braden's View

As I run down the path to the cave, I know I should've kept a better eye on my brother, but he'll be sixteen next month. Coda acts like a typical fifteen-year-old; he thinks he knows everything, but he doesn't. He seems to be possessed by the very thought of this cave. I can't stop him when he has his mind made up to do something reckless. Coda's curiosity and reckless abandon leads him into the world of adventure and intrigue every time. Bottom line: I'm responsible for him, and I've got to get to him before he hurts himself. In a way, I envy him, because he will get to see what's inside the cave. No one knows what's in the cave. Coda is like an addict—he has to get to the cave, even if it endangers his life. He imagines stalactites and stalagmites and a cavern big enough to drive through, like the ones we saw in New Mexico. I tell him that the rock formations in this area are alabaster, gypsum, and shale. The Carlsbad Caverns were limestone, and it's the decades of water seeping into the limestone that melts the minerals, forming the stalactites and stalagmites. I point out the logical reasons why that isn't what he'll see. I tell him it might be more like Alabaster Caverns near Freedom, Oklahoma.

I wish I could act without thinking everything through first. Coda acts first and then thinks about the consequences later, and he usually has a blast the whole time. He's always trying to prove that he's tougher, rougher, and smarter than me. If he just had some common sense to go along with all that bravado, he'd be unstoppable. On the other hand, I like to think things through, anticipate the danger, and weigh the pros and cons. By the time I've finished deliberating, the opportunity is past and the fun is gone—but so is the danger.

"*Aaaaaaaaa!*" A blood-curdling scream fills the air . . . and then another.

All Coda's laughter at jumping into things will never be able to erase the piercing screams and sudden silence the air now holds. I feel sick. I'm at the entrance to the cave, kneeling, looking into the darkness.

"Coda!" I call his name several more times, but there is no answer, not even a whimper. I should be able to see his flashlight's beam, but there is nothing.

I've got to get help. Mom won't be back until dark, and that's at least ten hours away. The nearest neighbor is a mile and a half, or I could run back to our house and call for help. It would take me about thirty minutes if I gave it my all. I don't know how long it would be before I could track someone down, though. I could call the county sheriff, but he's at least thirty miles away. We'd then have to come back and look for Coda. It might take an hour or an hour and a half, even if I find someone immediately. If only Coda would answer me, I could make a better decision. What should I do? I know what Coda would do if I was in the cave. He'd come after me immediately, no matter what. I know how afraid of the dark my little brother is, but that wouldn't stop him. I hate the dark myself. All I see now is total darkness. Whatever is to be done is going to be up to me.

I look around and find an oak limb about three or four feet long. Oak burns the slowest in the fireplace, so I'll use that for a torch. Breaking off the smaller twigs, I spy the remains of the legs of my jeans I'd cut off to make shorts for swimming this past summer. I keep calling out to Coda as I work, but I keep my tone soothing. I tell Coda I'm on my way and everything will be all right. I don't know if the reassurances are for Coda or me. I tear the jeans into strips, wrapping them around the oak limb I'd soaked in water. I know the strips will burn through and fall off if I don't secure them somehow. I think I hear a groan from the cave, and this kicks me into high gear. Sprinting up the stream to the top of the dam, I grab the backpack, first-aid kit, some baling wire from a tree—it was left in the cedars to tie tarps to it last summer—and the ten remaining stringers that Coda packed as a joke. I quickly fashion a sort of wire cage around the cloth, and I'm back at the cave in a flash.

"Coda, can you hear me?" I call out, with more panic in my voice than I want him to hear.

A moan is my reward. I'm sure I hear him. A kind of relief flows over me, because at least now I know he's alive. The sobering thought that he might not have been shocks me. I can't believe it was even in the back of my mind. Why doesn't Coda ever see that his actions affect more than just himself? I have to stay positive and not dwell on anything negative. I'm thankful that the weather hasn't been warmer. It has been cool enough for a jacket all day, and I'm sure the nights have hit freezing a few times already this fall. Colder weather means that the rattlesnakes would be moving a little slower now, if at all. I begin to think logically about all the things that can go wrong; for instance, the snakes may have moved deeper into the warm earth. I wonder how far inside the cave Coda managed to go. I take one last look around for anything I might need later, and I try to light the torch, but the wind keeps blowing it out—I have to crawl inside the cave to light it. I squeeze into the opening headfirst, and as I lay half in and half out of the cave, I pull my homemade torch forward and light it. It flickers; the stringy threads light but then go out. I try again, and it burns a little longer but goes out before I can even take my eyes from the flames to look around. *Third time is the charm,* I say to myself as I hold the match to the fabric, this time holding the match there until it burns me. The flame begins to crawl around the stick, following the torn threads. Finally, it lights! I can see a few feet at first, and then the torch burns brighter, and I can see more of the hole that gapes before me. My tear-filled eyes search everywhere, but there is no sign of Coda. I choke out another call as I hurriedly begin to crawl inside. There is no sound this time, not even the moan. My heart is so heavy that it seems it might fall from my chest.

As soon as I enter the hole, I can see that it becomes a little larger, and it opens in all directions to reveal several smaller, washed-out cavities.

I guess that the spring drained through here years ago, washing out this cavern. The ceiling isn't high enough for me to stand, but there is plenty of room around me. I check each one of the washed-out holes, holding the torch in one after another as I work my way deeper and deeper down a hall. The cave opens up until finally it is big enough for me to stand and walk. I've only just entered the next hallway, where I stand up, when the flooring crumbles. I move back against the wall and hold the torch lower. The hall opens into a pit-like cave. I'm on a ledge, and another ledge is about ten feet down, along my side of this opening. My light isn't bright enough to see the opposite wall.

I'm unsure how deep the pit may be. I shine my light downward—and I see Coda! I'm so relieved, I drop to my knees and call to him, but he just lies there, moaning. He has fallen very close to the edge of the dark emptiness. I can tell by the angle of his foot that at least one leg is broken. I hold the torch down in the opening, calling to him. As I study his lifeless form lying on a ledge, I think, *Only a few feet farther and he would've landed in the pit.* Then, before terror can take hold of me, I hear him moan. I begin to cry, releasing some of the tension. I wipe my eyes, and force myself to focus. My analytical mind flies into high gear. I quickly take in the whole scene: there's a hole of undetermined size and a six-foot-wide ledge wrapping around about twenty feet of the circumference. This is where Coda is lying. Beyond that, it's total darkness. I can't tell how deep or where the opposite side might end.

Coda moves. He's waking and rolls closer to the edge.

"Coda, lie still! Very still!"

It echoes through the cavern. *"Coda, lie still! Very still!"*

Coda freezes, and he looks up to the light flickering above him. A smile crosses his face, and he says, "Braden, what happened? I should've waited. I just wanted to be the first at something." He starts crying softly. "I can't move my right arm, and my shoulder feels awful. Help me, Braden. I want to go home. It hurts, even when I'm not moving." For a guy who is usually pretty tough, it's hard for me to see him cry. Even when he was hanging by his skin in the thorn bushes, he never cried. I know he must be in tremendous pain.

I talk calmly and seriously. "Coda, listen carefully. You must move closer to me and the wall, away from the edge. Can you crawl?" I ask.

Coda looks around, and I sense his panic. He tries to scramble away from the edge, but his right leg has a huge cut on it, and a bone is sticking out of his jeans. He screams, and I can only assume he's just seen the blood-soaked leg of his jeans, the bone, and the dark hole—but I can't decide if the scream is due to extreme pain or fear. Again, I calmly but firmly give my little brother directions. Every word we say to one another is repeated by the echo; it's unnerving.

"Coda, sit still. You'll be all right," I say soothingly. "We'll get you out and fix you up."

Even in the dim light, I can see he's staring and screaming at his leg and then at the edge of the pit and back again.

"Coda, look at me!" I bark. "Coda, *look at me*, I said!"

Coda's screams and frozen focus subside somewhat. He gazes up into the light of the torch with jerking sobs. I see Coda's head bobble as he tries to focus on me. It seems as though he's about to pass out. I quickly rattle off the next directions before he faints. "Coda, I'm going to hook these stringers together, and then you are going to hook the metal clasp—the part where you put the fish—onto your belt loop. Do you understand?"

Coda nods. I comfort him and rapidly connect the stringers, making a long chain. I drop it over the edge with one hand as I hold the torch over the edge with the other so he can see the stringer. It works; Coda has the stringer. He hooks it onto his belt loop and fastens it. I can see he's slowing down and everything he does is with a tremendous effort. Coda's sobs are getting a little slower now, but I don't know what will happen when I pull. Coda will have to try to help, and I'm afraid he's about to lose consciousness. Coda is slim for his age, but his weight is more than I can lift as a dead weight. *Why did I think dead weight? That's a horrible thought.*

"Coda, I'm going to try to lift you up now," I tell him. "You have to help me all that you can. You're not going to be able to hold your hurt arm with your left arm. You have to hold the stringer with that hand, and with your good leg you have to find footholds and stand when you can as you come up the wall."

"Braden, I don't . . . think . . . I can . . . I can't do all of that," Coda says weakly, appearing confused.

"You're always bragging about how strong you are and how you can do anything I can do. You can do this. I know you can," I say.

"Braden, I don't know . . . I don't think I can," Coda says as he tries to stand on one foot.

"Coda, it's like this: our torch is almost gone and then we won't have any light," I say. "You will have to stay here while I run all the way home. You have to do this and do it now. Ready? Here we go—it is going to hurt badly, but I know you can do it. Help me all you can, and I'll have you out of there in just a little bit. I have to lodge the torch in this crack so I can use both hands. You'll be in the dark for a little while, but climb toward me. Don't make any jerky movements. We don't want to pop the hooks open on the stringer. Here we go."

"I want to use the ladder," Coda sobs.

"There's no ladder. This'll have to do," I reply.

I hold tight to my end of the stringer and hook it to my belt loop, just in case I drop it. I turn and take two or three steps back from the edge. I find a crack in the wall about the size of my torch. Using both hands for a moment, I plunge it into the crack. Immediately, the cavern seems to come to life with a rattling noise. The echo makes it sound like snakes are all around us. I call to Coda. He's half screaming, half crying again, in terror. I know the snakes' den has to be inside the crack where I lodged the torch. I watch for a moment and notice for the first time that my torch is almost burned up completely. I only have this one shot to get Coda out. It better work on the first try, because I know as soon as the torch goes out, the snakes will be out to see who the intruders are to their home. They can track down their prey by sensing the thermal heat. They'll find Coda before I find someone to help us. I also know I have very little time before Coda passes out from lack of blood or shock. The cut to his leg worries me much more than his arm. I yell to Coda so he can hear me over the rattling that's now deafening. Coda's cries become louder every time the rattling does.

"I can do it! I can do it!" he cries out in fear and pain. "Let me . . . try . . . the ladder."

"Coda, we've got one shot. Pull yourself together. There is no ladder!" I shout. "You have to concentrate, focus on the top of the hole, and help me, on the count of three. One . . . two . . . three!"

I pull. The stringer pops and creaks but holds together. Coda is light. I send a prayer upward. *Please, Lord, let the stringer hold. Help Coda and me, Lord, to have the strength we need.* I see the top of Coda's head. I begin pulling harder. The rattling is slowing down, meaning that the snakes are on the move. That isn't the only thing moving! Coda's hook around his belt loop has become unhooked and is slowly straightening out. If it slips off, I know Coda won't be able to hold on tightly enough with one hand to support his weight. Coda is to the top of the hole, just about over the ledge to the hallway floor. That's when the hook straightens, jerking Coda off balance. He screams and falls back toward the pit. In the very dim light from the last of the burning jean strips, I can see terror in his eyes that he can't hold on. I leap forward and grab Coda's limp right arm and hang on. Coda screams in pain and faints—but I have him. I pull him over the side, hearing the crunch of cartilage in Coda's shoulder. Coda is safe, but the light is very dim and flickering, about to go out. The rattling has stopped. Where are the snakes? I glance at the crack and see one slither ever so slowly. Crawling, I shove Coda ahead of me until finally, I see daylight. I shove Coda out the opening first, and then I push my way through the opening. Coda is still unconscious from the loss of blood or the pain; I don't know which. I hear the rattling beginning again as I look back and see the last of the strips of burning jeans fall from the homemade torch. It lights the floor near the backpack. There are several snakes already slithering all over the first-aid supplies I'd brought.

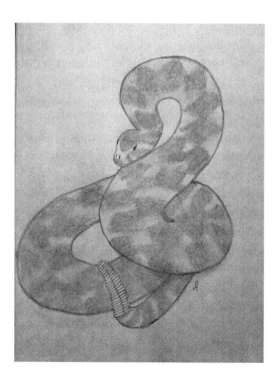

I can't do this, I think, panicking. *I don't know what to do. I need help, but the nearest person is a mile away. The only one with me is Coda, and he can't help.* A breeze blows past, and a Bible verse—Psalm 3:4—pops into my mind.

To the Lord I cry aloud, and He answers me from His holy hill.

I speak aloud, talking to myself. "I know God hears me. God got Coda out of the pit. He answered my prayer. I memorize verses all the time, but I don't really think about them being something real." I figure my subconscious placed the verse in my head. Another breeze blows past and another Scripture—this time Romans 8:26-27—comes into my mind.

In the same way, the Spirit helps us in our weakness. We do not know what we ought to pray for, but the Spirit himself intercedes for us with groans that words cannot express. And he who searches our hearts knows the mind of the Spirit, because the Spirit intercedes for the saints in accordance with God's will.

This is my mom's favorite verse, because when her brother was dying, Mom said she didn't even know what to pray for anymore. She prayed for wisdom as she took care of his affairs. She prayed for strength as she lifted him when he couldn't lift himself. She prayed for discernment to know which doctor to go to for help. She felt helpless but always relied on God through prayers, and this verse was pointed out to her on the day of his funeral. She has clung to it ever since. God told her through His word that she didn't need to know how to put what was in her heart into words. She just needed to believe with all her heart that when Jesus died for us, He left the Holy Spirit here to guide her—to guide all of us, really. The Spirit will help us with words when we have none. God knows what we need before we do, and He is already taking care of it.

I bow my head and pray because I realize it isn't my subconscious; it is God wanting me to know He is with me. *Thank you for helping me. Lord, you know my weaknesses. Please give me what I need to get us home.* I sling Coda over my shoulders and begin walking up the canyon path. Carrying him this way, I can hold his injured limbs steady and not jar them as much. We travel over the dam and through the pasture, away from the pond, faster than I thought humanly possible. I open the gates at the railroad tracks and leave them open. I can't waste any time. Coda's breathing is getting shallow, and I'm huffing like a steam engine. Man, I didn't know I was so out of shape. I'm now on the very sandy road that leads away from the pond. Each step is laborious. I sink into the ever-shifting deep sand.

I'm still in the thick brush and trees of the pasture and a half-mile from the house. No one will see us, even if they look this way, because of the trees. I must make it out into the open. I sink deeper into the sand with each step; it's an effort to walk. My pant leg feels stretched tight against my leg.

I'm getting short of breath, dizzy, weak, and feeling sick. I lay Coda down and realize my heart is racing, and I can't seem to get enough air. I look down and notice one pant leg is tight on my leg. I struggle to pull up the leg of my jeans. Some of my jeans have slits up the back so they'll fit over the tops of my boots; these jeans happen to be a pair with slits. Now, I pull at the slit on the tight pant leg until it rips. I rip my jeans up past my knee. Now I can see two puncture wounds—a snake bite. I remember feeling pokes and scrapes from the rocks as I crawled out of the cave; one of them must've been a snake. I try to remember what to do if bitten by a rattlesnake. *First, don't move or do anything to cause your heart to pump faster.* I've messed up already. My heart has been working hard to pump blood through my body, and with it has been the venom. *Second, band off the area of the bite, isolating the venom.* I pull the strings from our hoodies and use them as a band on each side of the bite, knowing I'm probably too late. *Third, sit down for twenty to thirty minutes, giving the poison time to localize, and keep the bite lower than the heart.* I should be able to walk on out then, but not while carrying Coda. I'll have to leave him. I know that is what I need to do. Coda is still unconscious, and his breathing is shallow. I can go faster alone, and we both need help now. I'll lie uphill with my leg below my heart and rest for twenty minutes. I put a splint on Coda's leg and tie my jacket around it, using the sleeves. I raise his leg onto a stump and place him on a mattress of leaves. I get sick again, and I'm really cold, so I lie down beside Coda. I'm breathing heavily and feeling sick again, so I roll onto my side. The world begins to spin out of control. There's a flash of bright light . . . and then blackness.

"I want to hear Ed's story again. Ed, will you tell us how you found Braden and Coda again?" Fuller asks.

"Sure, I was sitting there reading, and a bright light flashed and lit up the room," Ed says. "I went to the window to see if a storm was brewing. There weren't any storm clouds, but my tackle box was on the bench. I had this overwhelming urge to go fishing. You don't get to be my age by ignoring those strong feelings. I loaded up and headed to your pond. I found the boys lying there at the edge of the grass field. I loaded them up and headed to the hospital as fast as I could travel. I called your dad from the emergency room, and you know the rest."

"What was the light?" Eli asks.

"I don't know, but I'm glad it got my attention when it did," Ed answers.

CHAPTER 4

HOME, HAUNTED, & HARRIED

Braden doesn't talk to me all the way home from the hospital. I think he's keeping his eyes closed to ignore me. We were there three days. I've told him dozens of times that I'm sorry he hurt himself. He acts like it was my fault a snake bit him. I don't know why he thinks I have control over snakes. Mom says to give him some time. I think three days in the hospital is enough time. Now that we're home, I'm ready to make plans to return to the cave and get things back to normal around here.

"Braden, I can read some of your literature to you," I offer. "I know your headaches keep you from reading, but you could listen."

"I just want to sleep. Leave me alone, okay?" Braden says as he lies on his bed. He doesn't even look at me.

"Sure, I can do that," I answer sadly, because I didn't get to ask him about going back to the cave.

Alexa is walking past our bedroom doorway, and I call out to her, "Alexa, do you want to watch a show with me?"

"We're in the living room. I'll wheel you in here with us," she answers, pushing my wheelchair.

Braden and I do our schoolwork at home for the next two weeks. When we do return to school, I'm still in a wheelchair, but Braden manages to get around on crutches.

"Boys, gather your things. I'll need to take you to school for a while," Mom says. "The bus driver says they can't accommodate wheelchairs on the bus."

Not being able to drive just about kills Braden. It's his senior year, and I know he was looking forward to driving to all the extra-curricular activities. He was on first string in football but doesn't get to finish the season now, and they're in the playoffs. He lost quite a bit of muscle and had nerve damage from the rattlesnake bite. I heard Mom and Dad talking last night about how basketball is out, too. Braden can still go to the games. I don't know why he is moping around. The rest of us can't go to the games unless we're playing. Dad says we can't afford to go; there are too many of us.

"Braden, I'll be good as new by Christmas break," I say. "You will be back on your feet as well. How about going over to the pond and just peeking in the cave? I know I saw a ladder, and I can't get it out of my mind. I think I saw a feather, too. How would a bird get in there? Who brought the ladder, and where might it lead?"

Braden just looks at me like I'm speaking a foreign language. Or maybe it's a look that says, "I can't believe you asked that." He just shakes his head, goes to his room, and closes the door. It's really our room—the boys' room. I never thought it was quite fair that the boys have a room and the girls have a room. There are five boys and only two girls. Mom says that this is Braden's senior year, and if he closes the door for privacy, we all have to respect that and not go in for anything. We sleep there, but that's all. I've moved my important stuff out to the garage. I keep my things in an old ice chest, and I spend most of my time in the garage now.

The ladder and feather haunt me. I'm climbing old rope ladders in my dreams. The weeks fly by, and before I know it, it's Christmas break. Braden is still giving me the semi-silent treatment—speaking to me but very little. I tell him I'm sorry about what's happened to him, but I'm not sorry for going into the cave. His face gets flushed—it does that when he's mad—but he never says anything. He usually just walks away. I don't know why that makes him mad. I've got to talk someone into going to the cave with me. It's like I have no control over my thoughts of the cave. I must get back over there.

Liam is playing a video game, so I join him. "Hey, you've gotten pretty good," I exclaim. We were given this used Nintendo and a couple of military games years ago. Since it's the only one we have, of course we've gotten good at it.

"Thanks," he says, never making eye contact.

Liam talks less and less to the family. He is entering high school next year, so Mom and Dad relaxed their rule of staying in town without supervision. He met some guys through varsity sports. He never talks about who exactly he is with or what they are doing. He keeps to himself most of the time. You never know what he's thinking. Mom thinks he's shy. I think he's up to something. She thinks that hanging out with some guys his age will help him to find some good friends as he enters public school. We were all home-schooled through eighth grade, entering public school as freshmen. Mom thinks the preppy guys from the after-school program are nice. I know better and try to tell her they are chameleons. They let parents see what's expected and then do other things on the sly. Since I can't name anything specific, she won't believe me.

"How is that group of boys treating you?" I ask Liam while watching the screen. "Mom says you've been going to town to meet them a couple of times a week."

"They're okay. They let me choose the things we do after school sometimes. They actually value my input about the things we do," Liam says as he demolishes my tank.

I hear the edge in his voice. It seems he's been waiting to say that for a long time. Is he insinuating that they care and we don't?

"We care about what you think," I say, while avoiding his aggressive attacks on screen.

"Yeah, right. When was the last time you asked what I thought? Or better yet, tell me the last thing I said at dinner," Liam challenges me.

I can't tell him, so I change the subject. "Yeah, I like it when my friends like what I have to say," I add. "It makes me feel good if we use the idea I've come up with to solve a problem in science lab."

Liam knows I didn't answer him, but he graciously lets me off the hook. "Science? These guys like the way I think. They want to do things with *me* after hours. I can be myself, not some goody goofball! You better pay attention. I just cleared the field with one sweep, big brother! I just have to surround your bunker, and you're done for," he says, grinning with way too much satisfaction.

I step up my game a little and cut the chitchat. I know if the game is over, so is the conversation—along with my chance of getting Liam to go with me to the pond. Liam has revealed more to me tonight than he has in years. Well, to be perfectly honest, I never took the time to really talk to him. I know I never listen, but there will be plenty of time to fix that after I get to go to the cave.

"Now we're even again," I say. "I've gained back most of my power and weapons. You better watch out."

"Game over! I win! You're such a loser! I get a better game when I play Eli. I'm going to bed," Liam says as the screen goes white.

"Wh-what? Wait! What . . . what happened? Come back . . . back here," I stammer.

He used some sort of nuclear weapon and wiped us both off the map. Why would he use a strategy like that? Liam would rather kill both of us than lose—or was he ending the conversation? I didn't even get a chance to ask him to go to the pond with me. He's already to the bathroom with the door closed. He called me a loser! That's a lousy thing to call me. I think about it, and I realize he wasn't angry, just cold. I'll have to keep an eye on him. His response just wasn't normal. We've been raised to respect one another for our similarities and differences. This doesn't mean that we don't argue, fuss, and fight at times. We're family, but he seems to dislike me and the family. He seems resentful of being labeled as someone who chooses to say or do good things. There was the comment about not having to be a "goody goofball" when he's with his friends and now, he called me a loser! He hasn't heard any of the family use those words, so he's hearing it somewhere. I wonder where? Maybe it's the guys with whom he's spending time. But I'll worry about him after I take care of what I want to do.

The girls file by, going to their room. They've been studying together.

"Alexa, can you come to the garage for a minute?" I ask.

"Sure, I'll be right out. Let me put my books away first," Alexa answers.

While waiting on her, I think, *I have to get back to the pond, and I want to go over Christmas break.* I need someone with me because I'm a little uneasy about going back this first time since the accident. Later, there'll be plenty of time to find out what's bugging Liam.

As soon as Alexa enters the garage, the things that have plagued me pour out. "Alexa, I saw a rope ladder in the cave, and you'll never guess what else," I say, arching my eyebrows and adding a cheesy grin to pique her interest.

"I don't know. What?" she asks, flashing those incredibly deep dimples. We all have dimples—some of us have one, some have two. For a moment, I think I'm so lucky to have the cutest sisters, with their dimples and long, silky brown hair. But Alexa's dimples are the deepest, and when she smiles, like she is now, they give her such a wholesome look.

"Come on—guess!" I plead.

Alexa rolls her eyes, grins, and says, "You found a clay pot."

"Nope, I found a falcon feather! I picked it up as soon as I entered the cave, but I dropped it when I fell. What do you think a bird was doing in the cave?" I ask, hoping to stir her curiosity.

She sits down on an old bucket and states, "He was probably getting eaten by something."

I think for a moment and then I say, "No, there's no sign of an animal living there."

Alexa waves her arm for emphasis and says, "Well, maybe it blew in there."

Deep in thought about that idea, I say, "I don't think so, because the breeze blows out of the entrance. I guess it could've come from the other entrance, wherever that may be. I hadn't thought of that."

Grinning, Alexa stands, as if she is finished with the conversation, and says, "I don't know. What do you want, Coda? I know I call you a birdbrain, but what's on your mind besides feathers?"

"Since you mentioned it, I need to get back to the cave and check these things out," I say. Before she can say anything, I rush on, holding up my hand to stop her protests or flat-out refusal. "I know it sounds crazy, but I have to go. I can't sleep, because I dream about climbing ladders, and falcons follow me in my dreams." I yawn for effect. "I can just imagine the pieces of history we might find. It will make us famous!"

"I don't know, Coda. Ladders and feathers? That sounds pretty far-fetched. Dad said no one was to go to the pond anymore without him or Mom."

"Please, Alexa, it's important to me. I wouldn't ask you otherwise," I plead, using my best sad puppy-dog face and everything. "You don't have to go in; I just need you with me. I know how crazy it sounds."

"Coda, why don't you ask Mom or Dad?" Alexa asks. "If it is that important, you should be honest with them. They might go with you."

"Mom is always snowed under now, with Christmas and all that goes with it—gifts, food, and keeping up with all of us," I say. "Dad is working overtime to pay for the good stuff. I want a new controller for the Nintendo."

"Coda, you forgot the most important thing about Christmas," Alexa scolds me.

"What?" I ask bewildered.

"It's Christ's birthday—at least, it's the day we choose to celebrate our Savior's birth. You need to be honoring Him by thinking and doing things for someone other than yourself. We are His arms and legs until He returns." She shakes her head at me. "How can you ask 'what'? He gave His life for you. You have seen that kind of love, up close and personal."

"I have? When was that?" I ask, completely serious.

"Braden loves you dearly, and he almost gave his life to save yours—that's when!" Alexa exclaims. "He made a huge sacrifice. He did it willingly. He didn't hurt himself because of choices he made. *You* made the poor choices, and he loved you enough to save you. You're not even repentant for what you've done!" Alexa turns and stomps off toward the house.

Girls are so emotional. Alexa accepted Christ this year and is big on using words like repentance and sacrifice. *Well, I'll let her cool down and try again*, I think. I don't know what she's talking about anyway. I didn't ask Braden to come after me. I don't remember much because I was out of it, but he could've gone to get someone. As for Christ, I know it's His birthday, but it's not like we buy Him presents.

CHAPTER 5

FALCONS, FEATHERS, & FANTASIES

The cave is drawing me toward it all the time. I can't explain it, but I *have* to go. On the Monday morning after Christmas, I leave the house early, telling Mom I'm going to exercise my ankle. I get to the pond in about forty-five minutes. If the road was straight and paved like the highway, it wouldn't take much to walk there, but the pasture road winds and meanders around canyons and through sandy brush pastures. The sand is the worst. It pulls at my foot and adds more resistance. My heart is pounding; I can hear it drumming in my ears. Beat, beat, beat—no, it's the sound of wings coming up from behind me. The beating gets louder. Turning to look behind me, I wonder if the bird is going to hit me. It is gliding so low, I duck quickly, dropping to the edge of the canyon beside the dam of the pond. A small feather falls beside me as the bird dives and then soars up to sit in the top of a nearby tree. My leg hurts from all the exercise. My therapy gives me a workout, but this is worse. I should've warmed up and stretched out before taking off for the pond.

I sit and enjoy the nature around me. I can't resist picking up the feather. As I stand, I am bombarded with images of the cave—dim, muted walls with dark holes, a ladder, and a falcon. I guess I stood up too quickly, because I'm dizzy, and the trees spin, and the falcon goes round and round. As I stand on the canyon's edge, I begin to spin faster and faster, out of control. I fall, spinning down into a dark pit of blackness.

39

I come to a while later, cooled by the shade of a large cedar tree. I must've fainted. I remember bending down to pick up the feather and getting dizzy. I hadn't eaten breakfast and was light-headed from the exercise. I see the feather at the cliff's edge, but I'm not tempted in the least to touch it. It frightens me somehow. The feeling I had earlier is still with me—a sweaty, heart-throbbing, panicky feeling. I don't want to move, but I have to get out of here. I back away from the edge of the cliff, as if the feather might pursue me. I back into the branches of the cedar, and its prickly needles seem to grab at my pant legs. I look down at the ground and see large, brown, lifeless eyes looking back at me. As the hair on the back of my neck stands on end, the eyes of a buck return my gaze. He has small antlers, and as I pull back the cedar branch, I see it is just his head. A scream creeps up the back of my throat. I turn to leave, and the wind lifts the light falcon feather into the air. I stand there as if my feet are rooted as deep as the tree's roots. The beheaded deer is behind me, and the feather is before me, delicately balancing at eye level. Then the wind shifts and swirls and the feather flies straight for me. I backpedal into the cedar, which scratches my back and neck. The feather flies higher and higher and then away. I gasp for air; I'd been holding my breath. I scramble out of the cedar and stumble over the deer's head, saying some not-so-nice things about illegal hunting. One of my shoestrings catches on the antler, causing my other foot to stumble over it. It feels like the head rolls and tumbles between my feet, rolling forward with each of my steps. It's entangled with my shoestring. I start high-stepping, watching the head with its soulful brown eyes as it rolls in front of me, falling off the cliff. If I'd continued forward, I would've fallen too. I look over the edge, and I am directly above the cave opening. I stare at it, knowing I must enter—and enter it soon. If I don't, I know I shall surely go mad.

I hear the bird's call from the sky. I look up and see that it's a falcon. He circles and watches me. We watch each other for maybe fifteen minutes, and then I get uneasy. I ought to be somewhere doing something. I begin walking down the backside of the dam and head toward the cave. I'm being drawn as if I have no control over my feet. The falcon follows, getting closer and closer. The closer I come to the opening of the cave, the closer he gets. It's spooky. I'm so busy watching for the bird that I trip, and he dives at me. Maybe he has a nest or something, but I think it is the wrong time of year for nesting. He sits at the cave's entrance. I change my mind about the cave and head back. He flies to the top of a tree and watches me leave, calling as if to say, "Come back!" That's weird—he either wanted me to hurry along to the cave or to get away. Either way, I walk briskly all the way home. The falcon follows me but at a distance, calling ever so often. I get to the house, and I'm dying to tell someone about the falcon or the deer, but if I tell them, then I'll have to admit where I have been, and I'll be grounded forever. I settle for telling my youngest brother that there's a neat bird outside. Fuller and I sit on the deck and watch the falcon for a few minutes, and then Fuller wants to go inside and play video games with Liam. I remember when I was twelve—if it was my turn at video games, I wouldn't miss it either. I think I'll go with him. I really don't want to be alone outside with the falcon.

That night in my dreams, a falcon comes to me. The falcon is flying, and I'm outside. He comes to me, time and again, like he wants me to follow. I run to the house, but I can't run fast because of my stiff ankle. The falcon dives, and I try to put my right arm over my head to protect myself, but I can't lift it that high anymore. I wake up in a sweat and look around the room. Braden is staring at me in the darkness.

"Coda, are you all right?" Braden asks.

"Yes, I just had a nightmare; that's all," I say.

"Do you want to talk about it?" Braden asks.

I'm tempted to say yes since he is finally starting a conversation, but I say, "No, I'm okay now. Thanks."

He smiles and rolls over and goes back to sleep. I don't sleep for the rest of the night. I think back to the cave and the Indians that used to roam the area. I read that they think that dreams mean something, and birds have meanings too. I don't want to wait until tomorrow to look up Indians and bird meanings, so I slip out of bed and get on the computer. A quick search tells me that birds are messengers to the Great Spirit. I think Great Spirit is the title that Indians give to God. Then messengers might be angels, or it could be the Holy Spirit, because he takes messages to God too. But the Holy Spirit only arrived after Christ's leaving this world. I'm psyched about what I'm reading. I know I need to face my fear, so I bundle up in my heaviest coat, and I slip outside. The dogs follow me to the carport, where there's a lawn chair. I sit down and lie back, determined to think this thing through. I hear distant, rhythmic thumping. It sounds like a drum, but who would be drumming in the middle of the night? I bet it's Southard's gypsum plant. They're probably packing something, and the wind is just right to bring the noise over my house. I hear something else—it sounds like metal briefly scraping against metal. It's coming from the house. I slip around the end of the house, and I see our bedroom window screen propped up against the outside. How could that have fallen off? I creep closer and look inside. I can't make out for sure, but it looks like everyone is in bed. I look around the yard, which is lit by the nearly full moon.

I go back inside and find Liam's bed empty. It looks like someone is there because of the pillows, but he's gone. I open the window and poke my head out where the screen is supposed to be, and then it happens—it's like everything is in fast-forward and yet there are skips. A hand grabs my shoulder from behind me. I jump straight up, screaming—like a girl, of course—splitting my head open on the frame of the window. I double over, slumping out of the window because I dang near knocked myself unconscious. I mean, I know I'm not unconscious, because then I wouldn't know that my flannel pajama pants are coming off and are down around my knees. Someone is holding my pant legs to keep me from falling out on my head. I'm upside down outside the window, wondering what happened and how I got here. I'm kind of groggy, and I feel like things are in slow motion.

The dogs are barking and licking my face and the cut on my head, which, believe it or not, is making me more lucid. People are arguing in the house. "Pull him in!" "No, let him drop!" Well, the let-him-drop person wins, and I land on my head with my pants down around my ankles now. The dogs cover me with attention as I sit, right side up. Dad comes tearing around the corner of the outside of the house with his gun trained on me. I think I'm hallucinating, because he's dressed in his work boots, underwear, and Mom's robe. Mom isn't far behind him, wearing his work jacket and flip-flops.

"What's going on out here, boys?" Dad booms. "I thought we had an intruder!"

"I . . . uh . . . I'm not sure. Let me think a minute," I begin as I try to collect my thoughts—I know they must be lying around here somewhere. I had been outside, but I'd gone back inside, and now I'm outside. The dogs are standing on their hind legs, balancing on my shoulder to get to the blood that continues to flow from the cut on my head. "Oh yeah, there was a hand. Someone grabbed me on the shoulder. I got scared, and the rest is fuzzy."

"Get in the house, but put that window back together first! What were you thinking, taking the screen off in the dead of winter?" Dad barks and stomps briskly back to the front of the house. I guess his legs are a little chilly; I know mine are. I jump up, and my head throbs. I pull my pants up, attach the screen, and jog to the front door, also wondering why the screen is off.

Everyone is awake and in the living room. They're all talking at once, asking questions and making guesses about what's happening. That is the general conversation format for our family—with seven kids, it's the loudest one who gets heard. I notice Liam isn't saying anything, as usual. He's just standing there in his jeans and tied tennis shoes. Why would he take the time to get partially dressed?

"What happened?"

"Who broke in?"

"Did Dad shoot someone?"

"Why's Dad in Mom's robe?"

"Hush up, all of you!" Dad says, setting the gun back in the gun cabinet. "All right, boys, tell me what happened."

"I had to go to the bathroom," Liam says.

"I was asleep," Braden says.

"Me too," says Eli.

"Me three," says Fuller.

"Somebody was outside. I saw him through the window, out by the carport," Dad states. "I grabbed my gun and Mom's robe, slipped on my boots, but before I could get outside, I heard you boys and saw you shoving Coda out the window! Now, what's going on around here?"

"It was me, Dad," I say. "I had a nightmare, and I went outside to clear my thoughts. I was outside, under the carport on the lawn chair, when I heard something, like metal against metal. I went around the house and found the window screen off. I peeked inside and everything seemed okay, so I came back inside using the back door, but I couldn't find Liam. I opened the window and poked my head out to look around."

"I'll take it from here," Liam interrupted. "I came back into the bedroom from going to the bathroom, and I guess I surprised Coda when I put my hand on his shoulder. He yelled, stood up, and split his head on the window, and Fuller and I caught him, sort of, as he started to fall out the window. We had his pants, anyway. We decided he was more out of the house than in, so we let go, and he fell out the window."

"We weren't shoving him, Dad. Honest," Fuller says.

"For what it's worth now, I voted to pull him in," says Eli.

"Let me take a look at your head, Coda," Mom says and escorts me to the bathroom. By the time she's finished putting butterfly bandages on my head and we leave the bathroom, everyone has gone back to their rooms and is sound asleep. I thank Mom, and we turn in also. As I pass the back door on my way to my room, it hits me—I came in the back door. It was unlocked. None of us went in or out that door after Mom locked the doors for the night. I reach over and lock it, wondering why, tonight of all nights, Mom would forget to lock the door.

I'm calmer now. Nothing like knocking a guy out to settle a fella down. I think I can go back to sleep. I don't feel the need to stay up any longer, even though something still isn't quite right. Then I know what it is—Liam was in his jeans and tennis shoes but no shirt. Why would he get half dressed to go to the bathroom? Was he outside? Did he unlock the back door? I'll ask him tomorrow. As sleep blankets me, I wonder why the screen was off the window.

CHAPTER 6

TEACHERS, TUNING IN, & TRAIN WRECKS

"Dad, can Dulcie and I walk over to the pond and fish over spring break?" I ask at the supper table. I'm not hiding anything, and I ask respectfully.

"Coda, if I say yes, you cannot go near the cave," Dad replies. "I have to leave for the week and do field trainings in Santa Fe. You boys will have to be the men of the house and protect things around here. Your mother doesn't need more worries. I want you to act responsibly."

"I won't, Dad," I say and then hope I can resist it.

"You won't what? Go near the cave or act responsibly? I want to be sure I know what you're saying this time," Dad says, smiling.

"Trust me, Dad," I say, avoiding the question head on. It's one thing to hope you do the right thing, and it's another to say out loud, specifically, that you'll do the right thing.

"Okay, but be careful, and be back by noon," Dad says. "I want everyone home before dark this week. Mom doesn't need to round you guys up like a herd of cattle. You have to have your mother's permission before making plans."

I smile at Dulcie, but she glares at me. What's up with her? I figured she'd want to go to the pond over spring break. Braden told me he was going to be busy, submitting his last applications for financial assistance to colleges. So far, he has been turned down for all the scholarships he has applied to this year. Since he got hurt, all the sports scholarships have gone to others who are healthy. I can't imagine that filling out papers would take all that long.

After supper, Dulcie steps over to me, locks her arm in mine, and escorts me outside onto the deck.

"Hey, you're excited about fishing tomorrow, right? You don't need to thank me. Just let me catch the biggest fish," I say, smiling, thinking big sisters are sweet.

"Excited? Are you crazy? I have a date tomorrow night, and I was planning on fixing my nails and hair, not going fishing," Dulcie states.

"Well, I didn't know." I think of how nice it is to have brothers and sisters who always have your back. She could've blown my plan out of the water at the supper table, but she didn't. She didn't fuss about not knowing anything about my plan.

"Coda, for your information, you need to ask girls if they want to do stuff like this," she says.

"I thought you would like to go. If you don't want to go, maybe Liam will go with me," I say, letting her know there are other fish in the sea than her to go places with me.

"Liam is to help Granddad build an electric fence. Do you not listen to any of the conversations at the table?" she asks.

"I didn't know," I say. "I . . . well . . . I listen, but there is usually lots of other stuff going through my mind at the same time. I just don't always get the subtle conversations going on around the table when I'm eating." Everyone points out that I'm not aware of what they say, and that's getting a little old. You'd think I only pay attention to me!

"Coda, you are going to go fishing with *me* in the morning, and *I'm* going to give you an earful! You are going to start living up to your potential, so bring notepaper, pen, and your Bible. If you want, you can bring that rod and reel of yours too. This is the only way I'll go with you. You have to take notes and sincerely listen to me for half of the morning. Is it a deal?" Dulcie asks.

I want to go to the pond more than anything. I just have to get close to the cave. I might catch her sleeping and slip off and peek inside. I would've agreed to anything, so I say, "Yes. See you at dawn."

I go outside to pack my fishing equipment. I make a snack to take tomorrow—for both of us, of course. I can be a pretty thoughtful guy when I want something. Dulcie may sound growly, but she's harmless. *She won't make me study on break, will she?* I wonder. *I better pack my Bible, notebook, and pen, just in case she says she won't go without it. No sense in wasting time tomorrow gathering it together because I didn't do it tonight. I wonder what's on her mind.*

"Morning, Dulcie. I see you look as gorgeous as the morning sun," I say, showing her that I can be charming.

She rolls her eyes like she doesn't believe me and asks, "Do you have your Bible?"

"Why, yes, I do. Thank you for asking. I'd hate to forget it and have to come back to get it. Do you have your pole?" I say, smiling sweetly.

"Yes, let's get going," she says, while trying to keep from smiling.

She drives the family pickup to the pond, and she says we have to split the time between studying and fishing. I vote fishing first; she votes studying and wins, because she's eighteen and I'm sixteen. I ask you, where's the logic in that? We're all really close in age, about a year to fifteen months apart. In school, she is one grade behind Braden, and I'm two grades behind Dulcie. Alexa is between Dulcie and me. I look downstream longingly but open my Bible.

"Okay, Coda, I'm going to talk plainly to you. I'm not saying these things to hurt your feelings or anything. I think you need to know these things so you can become the leader for Christ that we all see in you. We all need to be prepared to do battle for the Lord. We need to know what we believe in so we aren't fooled. How can you lead others to Christ when you can't find your way out of a paper bag?" My mouth drops open, but before I can protest, she raises her hand and continues. "Here goes: you've been an inconsiderate dork to all of us but especially to Braden. We have the same parents; we live in the same house with the same rules. You attend the same church activities that we all go to, but you remain detached, not allowing a single thing taught to touch your heart—like service to others or repentance for thinking you're sinless when we all have sinned. You're smart, but you act like a smarty-pants. You think you have all the answers and if it doesn't specifically pertain to you, it's not worth knowing. You walk around like you don't have any common sense. You don't realize that your actions and words can actually be more harmful than a blow with your fist. You put two and two together but don't come up with four because you make your own rules. Those rules revolve around what you're interested in and what's good for you alone."

I look at her to see if it's my turn, and then I say, "If this is 'plain,' you may have to draw me pictures with captions, because I don't know what in the world you are talking about. Besides, everybody likes me just the way I am. I don't need to preach at people all the time to be good."

"Pictures? You need pictures? Well, here is one for you. Braden has paid dearly for your impulsiveness. He lost the use of his left leg. He's lost his possible scholarships in sports. He got so far behind in schoolwork this year that he is not going to make the cut to be considered for a journalism scholarship. No scholarship or financial help means no chance at college and a better way of life," Dulcie says. She loudly sucks in more air and starts again. "He has been planning on going to college for years. Making a statement like not preaching to be considered 'good' tells me you don't have a clue who God really is. You don't tell others who God is so you can get something out of it, like people thinking you're good. You do it because you love Him, and He has asked us to do this for Him. We reach out to one another and make sure—by our actions—that everyone we meet knows who Jesus is and why He came to earth. We're to do His will through service until He returns."

Dulcie couldn't get everything said fast enough. It was like she had been saving this stuff to spout out at me for quite some time. Well, it's not my fault, and I'm not going to let anyone make me feel guilty for something I didn't do. "I told Braden that I was sorry a hundred times that he got hurt," I say.

"There you go again, acting like *you* had nothing to do with it. It was *your* fault he got hurt in the first place. It wasn't an accident that *you* went in the cave. It was *your* choice not to listen to Dad or Braden. You say you're sorry he hurt himself, but you've never said that you were sorry you didn't listen, and he had to pay for *your* actions. You've never shown any regret or remorse for *your* actions that caused all this tragedy. All he has ever wanted to hear is that you learned something from all of this—that *you're* responsible for your actions and that they affect more than just you. Your decisions affect all of us. If you'd just learn that one lesson, then all that he's given up would be worth it to him. Your walk with the Lord is more important to him than anything, including a healthy leg or scholarships. We love you and want you to grow into the leader for the Lord that we know you'll be one day, but to do that you must know the Lord—I mean, *really* know Him. He wants you to repent of your sins, and then He'll be faithful and just and forgive them. We have all sinned," Dulcie says and then takes a breath.

"Who are you to preach at me?" I ask, getting more than just a little perturbed. "How do you know that I haven't repented?"

"I'm your sister, your flesh and blood. I love you more than you love yourself. I can tell you're not repentant, because your actions speak louder than your words. You only want what you can get us to do for you. Everything is for you and about you. You're selfish and prideful; you can't see past what you want personally. I'm sorry, but we all voted, and we decided you had to hear this from one of us. I just got the longest straw," Dulcie said.

"Well, sorry you lost," I snipe at her.

"Coda, I didn't lose; I won. We voted some time ago, and I've been waiting for the right time. This seemed like the perfect time. It's my privilege to share how much God loves you. I won. All of us who've made our confession of faith and know Jesus want that for you. We love you beyond measure. We voted to see who would *get* to tell you about salvation," Dulcie says.

"Who voted?" I ask, beginning to listen, finally. I think she really wants to help me. I didn't know that I needed help, but this explains why everyone has been giving me the cold shoulder and rolling their eyes at me all of the time.

"All of us kids, except Liam," Dulcie answers. "The vote was unanimous. Liam is in the same place you are. Perhaps one day, you will bring him to Christ."

"Even Fuller and Eli got a chance to vote?" I ask. "They're younger than Liam."

"Age has nothing to do with it. Fuller is wise beyond his years when it comes to knowing the heart of God. He and Eli accepted Christ last fall, when you and Braden were in the hospital. They've been praying for you every day. Have you felt something tugging at you, drawing you closer? Have you had unexplained things happen in your day? Did thinking about God or reading your Bible give you a kind of peace you couldn't explain?" Dulcie asks. "Well, that's their prayers at work."

I sit there, taking all of this in for a while. I can't believe Fuller and Eli have been so concerned for me. If I am to lead Liam to the Lord, I want to get it right. I love them, too. If all of them feel the same way, then maybe I'd better at least listen. I still don't feel like I need to change anything about me, but I don't want to be the last one to know I'm a dork either. It would be like a booger hanging out of your nose, and no one caring enough to tell you. I know Dulcie loves me and wants what's best for me. All of us kids might argue, fuss, and fight, but we love each other, and none of us doubts that.

"Okay, Dulcie, where do you want to start with me?" I ask quietly.

"I think you should find your own verses to lead you," she says. "Let the Holy Spirit guide you where he wants you to go. Pray for guidance to your repentance, and then listen. I think you could read these two chapters—Acts 3 and James 4. Then, pick out the verses that speak to your heart. Really learn it this time. Say it every day until it is a part of you. Don't just memorize words to forget them. You need to own these words, and hide them in your heart so that you might not sin against God. The five steps to salvation begin by first hearing the message, and then believing Jesus is God's Son, repenting of your sins, confessing who Jesus is, and baptism."

"You mean, read the whole chapter in each?" I grumble.

"Yes, the whole chapter, and then tell me which verse spoke to you and why," Dulcie answers.

She isn't all uppity about this or anything. She seems to sincerely want to help me. I begin reading, and it doesn't take very long. You know, when you're reading with a purpose in mind, like repentance, the words seem to make more sense.

"I'm ready. I chose Acts 3:19. *Therefore repent and return, so that your sins may be wiped away, in order that times of refreshing may come from the presence of the Lord.* And I chose James 4:8. *Draw near to God and He will draw near to you. Cleanse your hands, you sinners; and purify your hearts, you double-minded.* I chose them because they remind me I have sinned, and I'm apart from God. I need to stay close to His teaching, so that I know what to do. Is that right?" I ask.

"God spoke to you, not me," Dulcie reminds me. "The Holy Spirit will guide you to the correct understanding. Sometimes, it's simply what it says; sometimes it's implied. I think we should fish now. Last one to catch a fish cleans them!" Dulcie calls out, sprinting towards the pond.

I caught the first fish, of course, but I told her I would clean them because she needed to get ready for her date. I'm just a sweet guy like that.

"I appreciate what you're trying to do for me, Sis. Thanks. I may not have liked hearing it, but it needed to be said," I say.

"How about driving back for me?" she says, smiling.

I climb in behind the wheel and away we go. With seven kids, trying to get a turn to learn how to drive can be slim pickings. We only have the one farm truck, and we learn to drive in the pasture, where we can't hurt anyone. As I drive home, I think about my day and feel that it's been good. We have a stringer of fish for supper, and I haven't thought about the cave all morning. I'm feeling very good about myself—quite responsible, really.

We approach the railroad tracks, and Dulcie gets out and opens the gate. I pull through and sit on the tracks, waiting for her to close the gate behind me and open the one on the other side. The radio is blaring—windows are down so Dulcie can enjoy the music too. I'm singing and thinking about how wonderful life is when I see Dulcie's face change from peace to terror. She's opened the gate and is frantically waving for me to come across. I let the clutch out too quickly and kill the engine. The radio goes off—and that's when I hear the train whistle. I look up to see the train coming around the curve. For a moment in time, I freeze, not knowing what to do. All I can think is that if I die now, I won't be with my family in heaven, because I haven't made my confession of faith to God. *Please, God, keep us safe!* The train is braking but bearing down on me. I try to start the motor. Dulcie, her eyes wild, screams at me to get out and run.

The motor starts. I don't kill it this time and launch off of the tracks, stopping only after I've gone safely through the gate. I look in the rearview mirror and see Dulcie, frozen, watching the train. I jump out and join her. The air is filled with high-pitched screeching of metal on metal. The train didn't have much warning that something was ahead because there's a long curve. The train tracks are on a very old land bridge across a wide ravine, and it's steep up both sides to the tracks. This rail is used for hauling grain from Enid to the Gulf of Mexico. The train looks like it's loaded with grain, and that's causing stress on the rails. The rails give way, and as the railroad ties snap, there is a cracking and popping sound. The grain cars jackknife and then pull the other cars off the track with them as they tumble down the ravine, spilling their cargo down the slopes. The air is filled with a thundering crunching and banging of metal. The grain looks like waves of water, rushing and splashing as it hits the bottom and splashes up the other side. Metal on the boxcars bends and seems to cry out as the cars crumple to a halt. The engine comes to rest just past the road where we're standing. The ground here is flat, with just a gradual drop toward the ravine. The weight of the cars leaving the tracks pulls the engine and several cars behind it backwards, toward us. I grab Dulcie, and we run to the pickup. The engine has its brakes set and manages to stay on the tracks. The three cars behind it also remain on the tracks, giving it the stability to keep the engineers safe. Everything finally comes to a rest, and all that remains is the whooshing of grain pouring from the cars, along with creaks and moans as the metal collapses and the cars settle into place. The thunder dwindles to a low rumble and then is gone from the canyon.

"I'm sorry, Coda. I should've been watching and listening for the train," Dulcie says, grabbing me and holding me in a rare show of affection.

"I'm the one at fault," I say, breaking free of this awkward hug. "I've got to check on the engineer." I run to the locomotive. Two men—the engineer and a younger man—are climbing out of the engine as I arrive. I rush up to them, calling out, "I'm so sorry, sir! I didn't see or hear you. Then I killed my truck's motor. I'm sorry! Is everyone all right? Was there anyone in the caboose?" I'm trembling slightly.

"It's okay, boy. We're all right," the engineer says as he pats the younger man on the chest with shaking hands to confirm his words. "There aren't any cabooses anymore; there haven't been for years, just a little box on the last car that tells us what we need to know." He wipes the sweat from his forehead as he gazes at the wreck before continuing. "You couldn't have seen us any easier than we could see you. This is just a bad stretch here, but you know, in all of my twenty-seven years of conducting this here train, this is the first time I've seen a car crossing here," the engineer finishes, with a slight tremor in his voice.

I realize that Dulcie is standing beside me, and she is trembling more than I am—so much so that her legs no longer support her, and she crumples to the ground. The younger man is at her side and catches her just as she faints. He carries her to the pickup bed and lays her down, just as she is coming to.

"What happened?" Dulcie asks.

"You fainted, miss," the younger man says. "We carried you to the pickup. Are you all right? You've had a terrible scare."

"Thank you, but I think I'm all right now," Dulcie says, never taking her eyes away from the young man's eyes.

"I'm Coda, and this is my sister Dulcie," I say.

"I'm Engineer Roberts, and this is my new trainee, Rodney," the older man says, smiling at his young protégé, whose gaze is still locked with my sister's.

"Dulcie. That's an unusual name but quite sweet," Rodney says, smiling broadly. Most people don't know that "sweet" is the meaning of Dulcie's name.

I thought she might melt into a puddle again from Rodney's attention, so I say, "Do you gentlemen want to come to our house while you wait on someone to come and help you? I assume it will take a little while."

"That would be nice, yes," Engineer Roberts says.

We drive home, and I take the wheel again, because Dulcie and Rodney have decided to ride on the tailgate so the cab won't be too crowded. I'm mulling over in my head how I'm going to break the news to Mom. Dad said not to do anything to worry her. How am I going to explain wrecking a train? I think I'm going to be sick.

Engineer Roberts notices my worried expression and says, "Son, don't worry. We have insurance, and no one was hurt. It'll be all right. It wasn't anyone's fault."

"You don't understand. My dad's out of town, and I was to make sure things went smoothly while he was gone. How do I explain wrecking a train?" I ask with my voice breaking.

"I can explain that to your folks, if you want," the engineer says, sounding grandfatherly.

I breathe a sigh of relief. "Thank you, sir. You are too kind," I say gratefully. "I feel like the fault is entirely mine for not being more alert. I'd never met a train there before; I wasn't prepared." The verses from Acts 3 come back to me. [19]*Repent, then, and turn to God, so that your sins may be wiped out, that times of refreshing may come from the Lord . . .* [23]*Anyone who does not listen to him will be completely cut off from among his people.* Upon the heels of that thought come the words from James 4. [14]*Why, you do not even know what will happen tomorrow. What is your life? You are a mist that appears for a little while and then vanishes.* [15]*Instead, you ought to say, "If it is the Lord's will, we will live and do this or that."* [16]*As it is, you boast and brag. All such boasting is evil.* [17]*Anyone, then, who knows the good he ought to do and doesn't do it, sins.* It seems so clear to me now that this is exactly what I've been doing—boasting about knowing what's good but not doing it. I think that I'm not prepared to die either. I'll have to address both driving more carefully and where I want to spend eternity.

When we arrive at home, I stick my head in the kitchen door, saying, "Mom, we caught a stringer of fish for supper! I'll go clean them . . . and oh, by the way, we have guests." Dulcie and I guide the men to the kitchen table and offer them a seat.

Mom turns from making a salad, as does the rest of the household, who is sitting in the adjoining family room, to see who is here. I explain what happened at the railroad track, and Engineer Roberts adds his version, emphasizing that it was no one's fault. I sure hope she remembers that part when Dad calls tonight. I don't understand why calamities happen to me. First, the beaver dam, next I'm stuck in the thorn bushes, and the worst mistake, the cave impulse where Braden was injured, and now I single-handedly wreck a train.

CHAPTER 7

SENTINELS, SKILLETS, & SOCCER BALLS

Summer has arrived and with it, Dad has his bags packed for yet another training seminar. He has called all of us into the family room to tell us good-bye.

Dad places his hand on our shoulders as he addresses each boy. "Okay, boys, I need you to help your mom and take care of everything while I'm gone." He turns to Braden and me, making eye contact to make sure we're listening as he says, "I hate to leave you with this responsibility, but the money is too good, and with the layoffs, I'm lucky to still be working. I'll be gone two weeks, and then I'll be home for one."

As the eldest sons and sentinels of the house, Braden and I stand a little straighter as we match our dad's gaze. Braden speaks first. "Don't worry, Dad. We've got it under control. Coda and I are back on our feet, so we will be able to do more this summer. I'm so glad you were chosen to train the crew. They couldn't have a better team leader."

I add my two cents, saying, "Dad, I'll personally see to it that the grounds are kept secure until your return. Organization will be my middle name."

Mom keeps us all on schedule by saying, "Okay, boys, let your dad take off, or he's going to be late on his first day. He has an eight-hour drive ahead of him."

We all walk Dad to the car, wish him well, and say good-bye. It seems that I'm the only one who understands the importance of what

Dad is asking of us. After the train derailment, I sense there is something unexplained out there. There are mysteries, like the train derailment that prompted me to look closer at my life. I'm going to get to the bottom of these mysteries, no matter what, and I'll help take care of protecting the family. Braden and I can handle it. Braden has a job this summer, working for the local water-well drilling company. He hopes to be able to get a job with an oil field company after he has a little experience around drilling rigs. If Braden is too tired after a long day at work, Liam and I can handle the night shift. In fact, Liam offers to take the first night and every Friday, Saturday, and Sunday that Dad is gone. He's becoming quite responsible. I'm proud of him.

On the first night Dad is away, Liam slips out the back door after everyone is asleep, and I close my eyes, knowing we are in good hands.

The next night, we all go to bed as usual, but then I remember that no one is on duty.

"Braden, are you awake?" I ask.

"No, go to sleep."

"Braden, can I talk to you?"

"No, I'm sleeping."

"Braden, I think one of us should stay up all night and keep watch over the place."

"Good thinking. You're it! *Good night!*"

"Okay, I'll take tonight. Don't worry; you're in good hands," I say. I sleep in my clothes. That way, I'll be ready for anything. I won't let Dad down, like the foolish choice in the past—driving without a license. A man has to do what a man has to do. I think to myself that the family is in good hands.

I throw back my covers and slip out of the bedroom. I'm down the hall and out the back door without waking a soul. I sit outside under the carport, but it isn't long before I'm starving. I come back inside to see Mom, who's holding a cast-iron skillet over her head. She's in mid-swing, ready to take me out, when I fall to the floor, screaming, "*Mom!*"

"Coda!" she screams. She collapses to the floor next to me, visibly shaken by nearly taking the head off her sixteen-year-old. "What in the world are you doing outside?"

We look up and see several sleepy heads peering at us as we sit on the floor with a cast-iron skillet between us.

"No one told me we were having snacks!" Eli says, trying to wake up.

"We're not having snacks. All of you go back to bed," Mom says, and they all head to their rooms.

"Mom, you can just go on back to bed. I'll watch over us tonight. I just came in to get something to eat," I say matter-of-factly. I hop up as if nothing has happened and gather some peanut butter and crackers and a bottle of water. I step over Mom and give her a kiss on the top of the head as I swagger out the door. I think to myself, *It was an awfully pitiful swing Mom made a while ago. Thank goodness I wasn't a real burglar. Yep! It's a good thing I'm around.*

About an hour later, the crackers are gone but not the peanut butter. I share the peanut butter with Dancer and Roxie. Dogs sure are funny when they eat peanut butter. They start off licking and licking, and then they think if they raise their heads higher, they can get the peanut butter that's stuck to the roof of their mouth. They look at me like they love me so much. Tongues are flapping this way and that, and heads are bobbing up and down, as if they're in a very animated conversation with each other. I'm roaring with laughter at the dogs, laughing so hard that I'm crying.

Braden comes marching outside in his boots and underwear and throws a soccer ball at my head, grazing me. "Shut up! Get in the house, you ding-dong!" he yells. Then he turns and marches back in the house.

I wouldn't let him get by with that kind of thing if he knew what he was doing. I shake my head and think about how lucky I am that I don't walk in my sleep. I stretch out in the lounge chair and determine all is quiet tonight. I plan to just rest my eyes for a minute, but I discover the next morning that I'd fallen asleep.

CHAPTER 8

FALCONS, FLYING, & FOLLOWING

The rest of the summer was uneventful. The family went over to the pond as much as we ever did before the accident a year ago. Braden and I had a talk, and I told him I was sorry for not listening on the day of the accident. I told him that my actions had hurt him in so many ways, and I was sincerely trying to do better at not being so impulsive and self-centered. Nothing like a near-miss with a train to wake me up and realize I'm not walking the walk I want for my life.

"Braden," I'd said, "I'm sorry my actions cost you your chance at the scholarships."

I remember the true peace that spread over Braden's face as he said, "I can't honestly say I'm not disappointed, but I know that God is going to put me where I need to be, and He'll work through me. If it's an oil field job I'm to do, great. I can't think of a higher calling than to work for God wherever He places me." His example of faith was and still is inspiring to me.

"I never thought that what I do, I'm doing for the Lord. I mean, that someone might look at the choices I make as an example of Christian love. When I'm selfish, I don't want anyone to think that God is self-centered, because He's not; I am. I'll have to be more careful," I'd told him, thinking about the importance of actions that reflect God's intent toward others.

It's nice that Braden and I are talking again, and sometimes we have Bible discussions. Ours is a new relationship, more mature, and I like it.

I feel guilty, though, every day when he goes to work at the rig. Since my confession and ownership of causing his loss, I know it should've been me that was bitten. I should be the one to pay the price for my actions, not my brother.

Braden has a good-paying job, and it may take a few years, but he's saving lots of money so he can pay for school. I know his leg hurts at night, because I watch him rub it, and he gets up and walks around the room.

Tonight, I hear Dad encouraging him before bedtime, telling him to hang in there. "If you can get the money to go to school, then the oil company will consider you for some of the higher-paying positions. I'm very proud of you, son. I wish I could help you more," Dad says.

"I never expected you to help me. I will get there on my own, and if and when I do, I'm sure I'll be more responsible about taking this opportunity seriously. Dad, many of my friends have flunked out after the first semester. They just didn't see how important a college degree will be to them one day. I think God has used my accident to give me the perspective I need to do well," Braden answers.

"Always keep God front and center in your life, and He will see you through anything. I've got to get to bed so I can go to work tomorrow. Have a good week, and I'll see you on your days off," Dad says as he goes to his bedroom.

Braden has been staying at the bunkhouse with the other oil field workers to save gas money. The traveling is expensive when you figure in the cost of the gas and upkeep of the car. Without Braden's encouragement, I can't seem to get motivated to get my Bible out and study all by myself. I know I should want to study the Bible because I want to know what God says, but I figure I have plenty of time to learn all of that stuff. I'm too busy being young to worry about it now. The more I put it off, the easier it becomes to ignore it.

I need to get back to basics. I've heard the word of God. I know that Jesus is God's Son. I have repented of my sins and know that I was apart from God because of my sins. My next step toward salvation is to confess all of this, like it says in Romans 10:9–10: *That if you confess with your mouth, "Jesus is Lord," and believe in your heart that God raised Him from the dead, you will be saved. For it is with your heart that you believe and are justified, and it is with your mouth that you confess and are saved.* I don't know why I hold back on this step. I don't know why I can't talk to others about who Jesus is and share this good news.

I start having my dreams about the falcon again. He's flying, hunting, diving, and searching. By the end of football season, I'm sleepy, tired, and on edge. I don't sleep much, and the football practices wear me out. I've lost weight, and it shows in my tackles.

As I drag myself into the house after practice on this afternoon, Alexa says, "Coda, you have a phone call."

"Coda, fall break is next week, and I can't wait to check out possible hunting places for November. How about you?" Beau asks.

"Me too," I say, thinking to myself about the falcon and the cave. I have to go to the cave over break. It's with me constantly again. It had left me for a few months, and I thought I'd put those haunting thoughts to rest. I think sometimes I'm going crazy. Maybe if I confront my fears I'll be able to put these nightmares to rest. I decide not to tell anyone, but I've got to go back to the cave. I have to see the ladder for myself and discover where it might lead. Maybe I'm on a vision quest, like the ones I've read about in the Indian folklore. I'm more certain all the time that the ladder will take me somewhere, and the falcon is my guide. The farther I get from spending time with God, the greater the pull is to go to the cave. I've made up my mind. I'll leave early Thursday morning. Everyone will assume I have an early football practice and won't think a thing about it. I'll be back before anyone knows. My conscience is telling me that's dishonest, but I ignore it. I realize I've been ignoring Beau, too.

"Coda, are you there?" Beau says. "Hello, Coda, are you spacing out on me? Just tell me if you're busy. Don't leave me hanging."

"I'm sorry, Beau. I'm a little preoccupied. Can I talk to you later?"

"Sure. I gotta go anyway. See you tomorrow," Beau answers.

After tonight's extra football practice, I come home hot and exhausted. Coach always pushes one more practice in before fall break. After my shower, I open my bedroom window and find that Liam has taken the screen off again. I know he's the one doing it because I caught him one afternoon when he didn't know that I was watching. I don't know what that boy's obsession with taking off the screen is all about. I have a brief thought that maybe he's been sneaking out of the house, but my brother wouldn't do that, so I dismiss the thought. He's probably doing it to mess with me. I want to sleep with the window open, and I'm too hot to care whether there is a screen or not. There aren't any insects at this time of year, so I leave it open and crash on my bed.

My sleep fills with falcon images of the bird diving and dancing in the sky. He watches me and stalks me. I wake up, and the full moon is shining in the window. The room is cold, so I get up, close the window, and cover Fuller with a blanket—he's curled into a little ball, wearing nothing but his underwear. I return to my bed . . . and see a falcon's feather. Moonlight glistens off the spine. I look around the room frantically, almost certain that I'll see the falcon. There's nothing here. I double-check my brothers, and they're sleeping soundly. I pick up the feather from my sheets, and I put it in the pencil can on the desk.

Thursday morning, I'm up and out of the house thirty minutes before sunrise. I take the truck to the dam and sit inside, thinking about last night. I've brought the feather with me, and I twirl it between my fingers as I think. The sun crests the trees and shines into my eyes, waking me from my trance. I get out of the truck, carrying a long rope and a spotlight that is bright enough to light up a large area. I go straight to the cave. I hear the wind whistling through the trees. It almost seems to play a mournful melody. I feel a drumming vibration; perhaps it's the gypsum plant not far from here. The machines must be running, and the vibration is traveling down the canyon, matching the beat of my heart. I can't find the opening to the cave. I backtrack and search again, this time very slowly, examining the wall, step by step. I find the cave—but it's been filled in with rock and dirt! Who'd fill it in? I look carefully and realize that it's been filled from the inside—there doesn't seem to be any dirt disturbed outside. I head back to the truck and get a shovel and the hatchet. I smile, thinking about the beaver dam and Braden going after the same things a little over a year ago, when I was hanging upside down in the thorn bushes. I realize I haven't smiled in quite some time. As I start back to the cave, I hear the falcon. I put on one of Braden's hard hats and keep going. Let that crazy bird dive-bomb me; nothing is stopping me this time. I begin to dig at the opening, and I unearth some canvas. I stop. *What if someone is buried in there?* I look around and see no one except the bird. He seems content to just sit in the tree and watch me. I shine my light on the material; it looks familiar. I keep digging and pull out my backpack, first-aid kit, and the stringers hooked together into a long rope. How did they get in the fill dirt? Were they inside the cave? I don't remember.

The entrance is clear, but I don't want to enter it after knowing that someone else has been here. The fact that someone came from the inside spooks me. I leave the cave and load up everything, including the backpack, stringers, and odds and ends. I put these things in my special-treasures ice chest out in the garage, placing the other things that already were in the chest on top. My heart is racing, and I don't know why.

I'm deep in my thoughts for the rest of fall break. A part of me is disappointed that I didn't push through the excuses I keep having about going into the cave. I know I'll enter it, and it seems that I'm meant to be there, but every time I have peace of mind about going, I have a doubt. The excuses seem to keep me from my destiny. I can't wait for Braden to come home from the rig on Sunday night.

In my impatience, I meet Braden at the door on Sunday evening, asking him, "Whatever happened to the backpack and supplies we took to the pond last year?"

"I had it in the cave with us when I was trying to rescue you. I couldn't carry you and the stuff out. I just forgot all about them, so I guess they are still in there. Why do you want to know?" Braden asks.

"Oh, I've been looking for them and couldn't find them, so I wondered what had happened to them. It's not important," I lie as I contemplate who could've filled the cave.

Later, as we're having supper, I say to the family, "Has anyone picked up a falcon feather outside, maybe, and brought it in the house? I found one."

"No," the girls say in unison.

"Cool, Coda," Fuller and Eli say as they look at it. Liam pretends that I haven't said anything. Their answer leaves me with more questions than answers. If no one brought it into the house, the only way it could've gotten on my bed is by the bird itself.

I don't think it's cool. I think it's weird. It's strange. I begin researching falcons and the legends around them. The Peregrine falcon got its name because it migrates throughout the world, traveling great distances—*peregrine* means foreigner or stranger. The birds are very smart and accurate. The European cultures use them as warlike symbols. Maybe my finding the feather means I'm going to enlist and go to war. Falcons represent visions, power, wisdom, and guardianship. I wouldn't mind having some of those traits. They mate for life and return to the same nesting spot each year. Maybe a girlfriend is in the near future for me. I finally find a Native American website, and it says that the falcon's message is to be discriminating with my choices. I know I haven't made good choices lately. I've lied and been dishonest in my unexplainable need to see the cave. The website says I need to choose with accuracy and precision, and if I show restraint in my actions, I'll have success. If the falcon is helping me spiritually, it'll involve my path to God. I'll need to be accurate, so that means I've got to get back to the Bible studies. That's the only book that will lead me precisely to God. I know I need restraint with my actions. Because of my ADD, I've a tendency to jump on viewpoints impulsively, and I'm misled away from God's intent for my life. I think about them later, and that's a mistake most of the time. Maybe that's what I'm to learn. I like what the Indians believe about the bird. He doesn't seem so scary now. I think I'll make another trip to the cave over Thanksgiving break. My breaks from school are when my need to visit the cave seems the strongest. I guess it's because that is when I logically have the time. This next break brings with it hunting season, and everyone goes off by themselves to hunt in their favorite spots. My spot this year will be the pond, where the deer might go for water. I can't help it that the cave is just a short distance away. Accuracy, restraint, and success—those are some of the things that Braden and I were working on in our Bible study. Maybe God is speaking to me again. What did Dulcie tell me to do? Pray for guidance, and then listen for the answer. I bow my head and pray silently. *Lord, please guide me to You. You've provided Your word through the Bible to show me the way. Help me to stay focused long enough to see what You have to say. Romans 14:12—Each one of us will give an account of himself to God.*

I believe I'll be held accountable one day for my actions, and the fact that I've used my ADD to excuse myself from owning those actions will not matter to God. He knows me inside and out. He knows it's difficult but not impossible for me to concentrate. I feel like I've done a better job of staying focused and limiting my undisciplined random thoughts since I began my Bible studies. These changes happen as I begin to rely on God's strength and not my own. I believe God looks at how far we've come and not how far we have to go.

CHAPTER 9

DREAMS, DANGER, & A DUMMY

This is the last day of school before Thanksgiving break. My mind scurries from one subject to another, completing one before going to the next. I am doing better at controlling the bustling about in my head during school when I need to focus. I still struggle during my free time. I used to think I didn't have time to study the Bible, and what I found out is that everything in my day goes by more smoothly when I make time. It's my choice to have a better day by putting God first.

Later, at football practice, Coach says, "Okay, boys, no extra practices over break." We all cheer, but Coach puts up his hand, silencing us. "On one condition: don't overeat and puff up like toads, and please don't become couch potatoes. I want you to get some exercise. Now, have a great Thanksgiving and get out of here," Coach says, smiling.

As we gather our things, Beau tells me, "Coda, they've got the midterm tests posted. Let's go by the office before leaving school and check our grades."

"Sure," I say absent-mindedly. My thoughts are on the cave. I want to resolve this unrest that I feel. Something is lacking or incomplete. I feel stronger spiritually, but I'm not quite there yet.

"How'd you do?" Beau asks as we stand in front of the office.

"I got four A's and one B. I'm happy," I say, preoccupied in thought. I just can't put my finger on it, but something is lingering at the edges of my mind. I think it is something I have to resolve and it involves the cave.

66

"I made four A's and one B too. Are you going hunting tonight?" Beau asks.

"Sure, right after I check on some things at home. Are you?" I ask, but it feels too much like a lie. I know I'm heading over to the cave. The ladder seems to almost call my name. I don't feel right about what I just said, so I add, "Well, right after I check something out I'll go hunting." Now, I know I'll go hunting, because otherwise I'd be lying.

"How about spending the night at my house tonight?" Beau suggests. "We can stay up late and play my dad's Black Ops game. He has some headphones. They connect to the Internet, and we can talk to one another as the characters while we play. Plus, you can hear other online players too. It's so cool."

"Wow, that sounds great. Can I get back to you a little later? I need to get home and check on some things first."

"Okay, let me know as soon as you can," Beau says.

I already have the spotlight and ropes in the pickup. My brothers and sisters decide to ride the bus home with their friends, so I head straight for the cave. No sign of a falcon—that's good. No one has filled in the opening after I dug it out—that's even better. I stand before the opening and wonder if I'm doing the right thing. Before I change my mind, I flip the switch on the floodlight and crawl into the first hall. The floodlight shines all the way to the back wall. No sign of snakes. I watch my step this time, aware of where I put my feet and what is all around me. I get to the part where I can stand completely. First, I have to see where I fell. I look down and see a ledge leading almost all the way around a pit. The pit does have a bottom—it's about another twenty-five feet down from where I'm standing. I bring the light up the walls slowly, and I see that the pit follows a vein of rock. It has been chipped away with something. My line of sight travels up a little farther, and there it is a rope ladder with rungs made from branches. That is how someone climbed down to the pit to chip the rock. I shine the light to follow the rope up until it is about five feet above my head. It looks like there is another opening. Of course! That is the way they came in and down the ladder. Who were they? I wonder how long it's been since anyone has been to this cave. Well, I know the answer to that—recently, because someone blocked the entrance. I can't get to the ladder from here. I have to be on the lower ledge. I'll need my rope. I step outside and see the sun is going down. It is too late to go hunting, and my family will worry that I'm not home from school yet. How could

I have lost so much time? I better go home and come back tomorrow. I only hope that Beau doesn't call the house. I sit in the pickup and watch for deer until dark. Then I head home as fast as I can travel.

Bursting through the kitchen door, I call out, "Mom, I'm sorry. I lost all track of time. It was so close to dark that I stopped off at the pond and watched for deer."

"No one else is home from hunting. It's only the girls and me," Mom replies calmly. Her sweet demeanor brings peace to all of us, especially me. She continues, "You are the first of the hunters to arrive, so I guess technically you're early."

Quickly I ask, "Beau invited me over to play a new game that his dad bought. Can I spend the night?"

"That sounds like fun. I think you should go, and I'll see you when I see you. You boys may want to sleep in or hunt tomorrow," Mom says knowing that I'll want to go hunting.

I give her a quick hug and say, "Thanks, Mom. I'm going to head on over, if that's okay."

"Sure. Your dad and brothers will be glad to eat your part of supper," she says, smiling.

I kiss Mom on the cheek, grab a couple of things, and then I'm out the door. As I drive, I think about tomorrow. I know it'll be easier to get away from Beau than from my family—he'll be sleeping. Guilt follows me out of the house, along with my dishonesty. Mom doesn't deserve that, because she trusts me. She deserves honesty and more.

Beau and I play Black Ops until about four in the morning, and then his dad tells us we have to quiet down or go to bed. We choose bed. Before Beau lies down, I ask him if he wants to go hunting in the morning, but he says no and is asleep before his head hits the pillow. I've been getting by on two or three hours sleep for quite a while, so I wake up about six-thirty. I leave a note that I've gone hunting and I'll call later. I slip out and drive to the pond.

My heart is racing with excitement. I pull up to the pond, park the pickup, and then decide that I might need to think about this. What do I know? Someone has been here besides me. I might want to take something to defend myself, in case whoever I find isn't friendly. I put my hunting knife in its sheath on my belt. Who would want to remain hidden in a cave? Robbers, maybe? Runaways? But if someone ran away in our small community, everyone would know. We know everyone by name. The cave could be a meth lab! Now, that was possible. I'll stay alert for the sights, sounds, and smells that they told us about at the school assembly.

I prop the spotlight on the opening above me. It should burn for a few hours before dimming. I check my two small flashlights and put them in my pockets, freeing my hands. I'd hate to get stranded in there in the dark; no one would know where I am. I shake the uneasy feeling, climb down to the ledge below me, and work my way around the pit to the ladder. I look at the way the pit has been chipped. It seems to have been a quarry. The rock looks like flint, so maybe the miners made arrowheads or tools. I test the ladder by reaching up, holding a rung, and lifting my feet off the ground. I hang there, suspended, for a minute. The ladder's jute-like rope creaks as it stretches, but it seems solid. The rungs are made of thick oak and don't show rot. I begin to climb, rung by rung, out of the quarry pit, pretending to be a young Indian brave who's finishing his work for the day. I pretend I've quarried several arrowheads and one larger chunk of stone to work on in my teepee tonight. I smile at the thought of going hunting with arrowheads. Being serious all the time has its advantages for focusing, but for having fun, a good imagination can't be beat. As I make my way up the ladder, I wonder where my Indian home might've been. I love imagining I'm someone else. I like to put myself in his moccasins, and as I pull myself to the next hallway, I've completely lost Coda, and now I *am* that young Indian brave.

The ladder is secured around two buried boulders. Braden was right about the cave—it doesn't have stalactites or stalagmites. It has water-washed pathways and tumbled rocks. There also are natural cavities. I walk on silently in my pretend moccasins, feeling the small pebbles underfoot. The first time I have to choose between two paths to follow, I notice some notches carved into the top of one path opening. I choose that one. I'm getting into my new character now and have chosen the path with the notches that my ancestors left to show me the way. I follow a maze of tunnels that seems to travel downhill and to my left, which is north. I walk for about half a mile or farther, when a musical breeze that has been pushing past me becomes louder. It seems to hurry along on an errand of urgency, blowing my hair back at times and cooling my skin.

I know I'm heading toward an opening because of the melodious breeze brushing my face. Maybe the whistling of the wind sounds like a melody to me because of my romantic notions of stepping back in time.

As I walk, the melody becomes more defined. I realize it's not the wind; it's a flute.

I wonder if meth-makers play flutes while working. My hand instinctively goes to the knife in its sheath. All of my senses are on high alert. I smell nothing but a little campfire smoke. I round a corner and come into a large, quarried room of gypsum. The quarried cavern has large pillars of natural rock, left behind to support the roof. The room is like one of the original old tunnels made by the gypsum plant. It was mined by hand—I know this because my dad took me to one that looked like this on the other side of the quarry, before they blasted the openings closed. I guess they missed securing an opening somewhere.

I continue to hear a flute, but the musician is behind the pillar that supports the ceiling. I maneuver around the pillar slowly. The tune is mournful and sweet. Who is playing this enchanting melody? The room is lit by a small campfire. The alabaster walls reflect the dancing firelight and make the room lighter. I switch off my flashlight and step around the pillar to see who is playing the flute—and I see the most beautiful girl I've ever seen in my life. Her skin is the color of milk chocolate. Her hair falls in gleaming black sheets across her back and shoulders. It is blunt cut, straight across at the bottom. She is wearing a long-sleeved buckskin dress of light beige. It is belted and ends just below her knees. As she kneels on a large, furry brown rug, her knees barely catch the end of the dress. Her posture is as straight as an arrow, and our band director would be proud of her arm and hand placement on the flute. I haven't seen her face yet, but her beauty and obvious grace are breathtaking—and I know what breathtaking means for the first time in my life. It means you forget to breathe, and you get light-headed, because I just did.

I want her to know I'm here without scaring her to death. I know I've already waited too long to say something. I feel panicky, and a cold sweat beads up on my forehead. Maybe I should just go back the same way I came and not say anything. She stops playing and stands. I know I'd better do something quick, but my feet are as heavy as a ton of bricks. She starts to turn, and I watch as if every movement is in slow motion. I want to remember this moment forever. I think I'm going to faint—how embarrassing! I think, *Breathe, you fool! You're holding your breath again.*

She looks at me. Her eyes are dark, with gold flecks around the iris. I tell myself, *Say something, you idiot. Give her a compliment!*

"Your hair is black," I say. Did that come from my mouth? Oh, my gosh! I sound like I'm in kindergarten—hair, black; walls, white.

Eyes dark as the night, now with tiny angry golden fireflies, stare back at me. I feel awful to have caused this elegant Indian princess any concern. She has the prettiest eyes I've ever seen, so with a tongue as thick as molasses I say, "Fireflies are pretty." I'm sweating, and I can't talk. *What's wrong with me?*

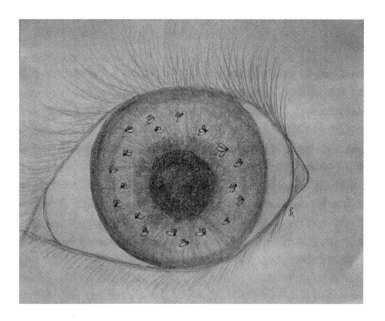

She whistles and crouches into a defensive position, grabbing a large stick from her wood pile. She obviously thinks I'm a threat and is going to club me.

I can't help but scan her body. Her deerskin dress has fringed edges around the bottom, with intricate beadwork across the top half of the shirt and belt. She has on knee-high moccasins, fringed at the knee and beaded across the top of the foot.

I'll make a connection this time, if I can catch my breath. I say, "I'm wearing moccasins too." *What am I? Ignorant? I'm not wearing moccasins!* I have on tennis shoes; the moccasins were in my imagination. Maybe she's in my imagination too. I hope so, because I'm so embarrassed, I could just die. I finally meet the girl of my dreams, and I'm dumbfounded.

She glances at the opening of the cavern, and I follow her gaze—just as I'm hit in the head by a dive-bombing falcon. The room spins, and then the lights go out.

"Wake up! Wake up," she says, poking me with the club.

It is my turn to be frightened. I say, "I'm sorry! I'm sorry I frightened you. Don't hit me."

She keeps the club aimed at my head but doesn't swing. "Are you touched in the head? Are you mentally challenged? Who are you? How did you get here?"

"No, I'm not touched or crazy. My name is Coda, and I came from a tunnel over there." I point to the back of the room.

She raises her club. "There is nothing back there except the pits. You lie!"

"No, it's the truth. My brother and I found an opening a year ago last summer, and I just now explored it. I didn't know this is where it would end." I rub my head and tear my eyes from the dark eyes that have mesmerized me to look closely at her. "Who are you? Where did you come from?"

She studies me, furrows her brow, and asks, "You were the ones to wake the snakes last fall, weren't you?"

"My brother and I were here in the fall and had an accident in the cave with some rattlesnakes. How did you know that?" I see her slender fingers loosen their grip on the club after hearing my answer.

"My name is Falcon Feather; my friends call me Feather. I heard you and the snakes. They scared me. I explored the tunnels myself in the winter. I found the pits and your opening. I closed it so you would not awaken the snakes again. You did not bring them with you, did you?" Feather watches me carefully with those firefly eyes as she answers.

I wonder if she feels this immediate, intense connection that I feel. It is as if I've found my better half. I feel completed being near her, and I want her to know I'm so glad to meet her. "No, I think the snakes are gone or sleeping. I dug the opening out to explore the cave. It is nice to meet you, Feather." I reach out to shake her hand. She reaches forward to take my hand in friendship, and I wonder if electricity will leap from our fingertips before they touch. A falcon appears, screeching at me and diving again. I yank my hand back and curl into a ball. I feel embarrassed that I've shown such cowardice in her presence.

Feather puts her arm out, and the bird lands on it. She tethers a leather strip around its leg and feeds it some meat. She carries the bird to a perch, close to the mat where she was sitting earlier, and ties him to it. She seems to notice my fear, but her only comment is, "Let me doctor your head."

I just sit there like a hound dog, with my tongue hanging out. I have a knot on the back of my head, where I fell on the rock floor, and a scrape across the side of my head, where the falcon clawed me. She brings a polished, obviously handmade gray clay bowl. The contents smell like cedar, and it feels cool as she strokes her beautiful, long, slender fingers across the cut. The mixture she uses may be cool, but my temperature is definitely rising. The mixture doesn't sting, but with each touch of her fingers, I feel a tingling. She digs around in a leather pouch and finds a T-shirt and starts tearing it into strips.

"Isn't a T-shirt a little out of century for you?" I ask, smiling. I hope she knows I'm teasing and not making fun of her.

"Yes," she says, smiling back. "I don't always wear my traditional dress, only when I think I am alone."

"Your bowl is quite unusual," I say forcing myself to think of something other than how nice it would be to get to know Feather better. "Did you make it yourself?"

"It's a family heirloom," she states simply, but I can tell she is flattered or proud that I noticed its uniqueness.

"I'm sorry again for intruding," I say, needing to hear her voice again. "I heard the enchanting flute music, and it seemed to draw me here."

Her head snaps up, and she stares deeply into my eyes, as if she is trying to read my mind.

"What's wrong? Did I say something to alarm you?" I ask, afraid that she might run away, because she reacted with such shock.

She leans forward and seems very interested in our conversation, saying, "No. Tell me more about why you came to this cave."

"You'll think I'm crazy!" I exclaim, thinking about the supernatural pull that has drawn me to this moment in my life.

"No, I won't, but I must know," she prods.

"Short version is that I feel like this cave is a magnet, and I'm a piece of metal. I'm constantly being drawn to it, against my better judgment," I confess, realizing for the first time how totally obsessed I've been in my pursuit to get inside this cave. Mom was right when she said I was consumed with the very thought of the cave. It's such a shock to see this in myself.

Now it's her turn to be unsteady. She sits down in front of me and stares for a moment before saying, "I'm here on a spiritual vision quest. I came to pray for wisdom and guidance. I had a dream, and in it the Great Spirit told me to play my flute, and the guide to the wisdom I seek would hear it and come." There is less of an echo in this room, but her words—hear it and come—seem to resonate off of the white hand-hewn walls and ceiling.

Now both our mouths drop wide open. I don't know what to say. I look at the falcon and then at Feather, dressed in her traditional buckskin, and wonder, not for the first time since seeing her, if she is a ghost. I ask hesitantly, "Have you been here . . . at this place . . . before?"

"Yes," she says. "I have been here at breaks from school and at the end of summer." She eyes me alertly. "Grandfather has been coming to this cavern for a few years now. The last time he came, he had a vision of the last terrible shaking of the earth—this means a war large enough to end the world as we know it will happen. This war may be about to begin. The signs of our tribe's prophecies have been coming true at a rapid rate. My people believe the end of times is upon us and that we'll need many Faith Keepers—people who accept the call of the Great Spirit—to remain peaceful and calm, while gaining spiritual enlightenment and understanding. They must be ready to serve and stand strong in their knowledge, no matter what our tribe endures. If the tribe is faced with extreme circumstances, they will need their Faith Keepers to talk to the Great Spirit and remain calm. I'm on such a quest to be a Faith Keeper."

My words tumble out rapidly. "My family also believes we're seeing many of the end time's prophecies coming true. Our Bible tells us that we'll not know the exact hour, but when we see these things coming true, we should be watchful and prepare for Jesus to return."

Because we're sharing such an intimate moment, I'm moved to reach out and hold her hand. Her eyes glisten as she continues, "My grandfather's vision revealed that we'll endure intense sufferings. We must be ready to meet them if we're to survive."

I caress her cool fingertips to comfort her but also to reassure myself that she is real, and I'm not imagining all of this. "The book of Revelation reveals the same sufferings to those who are lost," I say, parroting what

I've heard my preacher say at church. "It will become horrible for those left behind at the end. I personally believe God will come and get his followers first, and we'll not have to go through the worst part, but even if we do suffer, we must remain faithful." I surprise myself with how easy it is to talk to this stranger about God. I surprise myself with how much I remember from the sermons.

She moves slightly closer and strokes my fingers absently as she concentrates on my face and says, "Grandfather says that he saw a black hole in his vision. It was like a big picture, and there was something missing. My messenger is to come and tell me the missing piece. It will assure our everlasting; otherwise, we will become no more." She stops stroking my fingers and firmly holds my hands in hers before she continues. "My life has been full of distractions up to this point. I'd fill my days with my animal friends and schooling. These are good things, but I would make no time to meditate on what the Great Spirit wants me to do."

I blurt out, "I feel the same way. I've intended to do my Bible studies, but life just keeps getting in the way. I always think that there is tomorrow. I'm sorry—I interrupted you; that was rude. Please continue." I would've used a hand to clamp across my mouth to keep it closed, but I'd have to let go of her hands.

She lets go of my hands and begins to pace the floor. "My grandfather raised me." She pauses beside the falcon and then continues. "He named me after a falcon feather that fell from the sky the night I was born. I trust my grandfather. He is never wrong and is a strong spiritual leader in our tribe. Many believe our tribe is extinct, but we are many. He believed we needed to make this vision quest to this place, which he saw in his vision. We found it while visiting friends one year. Our tribe has always been drawn to unique natural rock structures, but this one is both man-made and made by nature. I feel the Great Spirit has led me to an understanding of spiritual enlightenment while meditating in this place. My people will need to remain calm and at peace, knowing that the Great Spirit is in control, no matter what hardships the tribe must endure. I've been coming here at every break from school since my sixteenth birthday in May of last year. In my vision"—she gazes to the ceiling before continuing—"I'd have a messenger and a guide." She looks straight across the room to where I'm now standing and asks, "Are you what I've been waiting for, Coda? I've been calling you with my flute. I sent my falcon to find you, but you did not come. Why have you tarried so long? Have you been preparing yourself?"

I feel like she is expecting a profound answer, and I don't have one, so I begin with what I know to be true. "I have to confess. I came to the cave that summer. I found a beaver's dam, which led me to finding the cave entrance."

It's her turn to excitedly interrupt the conversation, and she asks, "Yes, brother beaver was in my vision that summer. Did he not show you the way to me?" The hair on the back of my neck stands straight up. What she's saying is matching everything that has been drawing me to this place. The beavers blocking my path to all directions except the cave's opening in the wall made sense now.

I continue slowly, trying to process what I'm saying with the new information I've been given. "I came back in October of last year. I had to enter the cave, no matter what! In my rush to see the cave, I fell and broke my leg and arm. My brother was bitten by a rattlesnake, and it left him crippled. I should've been the one bitten, because it was my impulsiveness that caused the accident. If I'd only waited until it was colder, we would've been safe. I saw the ladder and the falcon feather in the pit where I fell, and it has haunted me until today. I dreamed of climbing the ladder. I felt it would lead me to somewhere I needed to be. I saw the falcon in my dreams most nights. The only time I rested in peace was when I did my Bible studies," I say, not just as a statement of fact but as a revelation for me. "I found a falcon feather on my bed in October when I left the window open. I made plans that on my next break, I'd explore the cave. That brings us to today." I search her eyes. Somehow the golden flecks are not the distraction that they first were, and it seems like she is a friend I've known all of my life. We are comfortable with each other. There is a satisfying familiarity to our friendship. As intense as our first meeting was moments ago, I now sense, just as intensely, that our futures will be entwined. I'm content to just sink deep into her soul as I hold her gaze.

She returns my gaze, slowly walks toward me, and says, "In my vision, the serpent would battle the messenger. He would stop the messenger from giving us the missing piece to our security. The serpent would strike and wound the messenger but not stop him. Grandfather said that there was a missing piece to the prophecies. Without it, the serpent will win; with it, the tribe will know peace at last. This knowledge will be revealed to the Faith Keepers; there are many of us. We are to take the message back to our people. You are the one I've been waiting for. What's your message for me?" she asks in a matter-of-fact way.

She is standing so close to me, I can smell the faint fragrance of cedar. The freshness of the aroma seems to fit her. She deserves the answers she seeks. Why have I waited to learn all that I could about the future and what my role should be in it? "I don't know what message you're talking about. I've been on a spiritual journey myself," I admit and then quickly add, "I can tell you what the Holy Spirit has revealed to me through the Bible."

"Tell me then, messenger," she says, waiting expectantly.

I can almost see the burdens on her shoulders lighten at just the thought of my having the answer she seeks. I feel guilty as I say the only thing that I can: "I'll need my Bible. I'll go home and get it. But because it's getting late, I won't be able to return until tomorrow."

"No! Coda, I must have your message as soon as possible. Please! I've waited so long already. Stay with me and tell me what I must know," she pleads, with genuine worry written all over her beautiful face.

I begin to walk back toward the narrow crack in the tumbled rocks where I'd emerged from earlier. I say with as much conviction as I can muster, because I can hardly bear to deny Feather any request, "I must go home so that I don't cause any worry to my family. They wouldn't let me come back. If I don't return, it's because I can't. I'll draw you a map to where I live. Here is my name and phone number. You come to me if I fail to return. Otherwise, if at all possible, I'll be here by sunrise. It's been an unexpected pleasure to find you here, Feather. I hope we can find many more hours to talk. I find you fascinating."

"I will wait, but my grandfather is to return and take me home soon, so our hours are numbered," she says. "Please hurry back. I would like to spend as much time as I can with you, too." Then she adds, almost as an afterthought, "My people have waited so long already, and I must prepare."

I start back through the tunnel, my thoughts consuming me. If what Feather says is true, God wants me to share the steps of salvation. I'm ready to be baptized, but I don't feel confident about being responsible for telling someone else what I've learned. I must make my confession of faith, acknowledging who Jesus is, and tell Feather. Why have I delayed learning all that I could? I feel confident in my knowledge, and my heart is at peace that I could speak boldly of God's Son. I need to get home and study. I pray that tomorrow it will be God's words and not mine.

CHAPTER 10

THE MESSENGER AND THE MEANING
OF THE MESSAGE

I drive home and find Dad and Braden in the garage, dressing out a deer. I join them, and they give me a hard time about hunting for two days and coming up empty-handed. I enjoy their company and bantering more than I can express. I appreciate my family more than I ever have in my life. Just knowing that what the preacher has been saying—that the day may be soon upon us when Jesus will return—makes me love everyone and everything about my life just that much more. I play a game of UNO with Fuller. We invite Liam to join us, but he wants to play video games alone. He's mainly texting someone on Braden's new cell phone. He's retreating from the family more every day. I have to reach him somehow and see where his head is, for sure. I've wasted time, and again, I may not be the one to pay for my actions—or in this case, my inaction. I know where Liam's been spending most of his free time, and I don't like it. His mouth reflects what he hears and sees when he's away from home. He's short-tempered and finds fault with all of us. It's always our fault, never his. It wasn't too long ago that I felt and acted the same way.

I need to take him fishing, like Dulcie did for me, but he doesn't like to fish. If we go to a game, all of his friends are around, and he disappears shortly after we arrive. I see now that I'm to witness to both Liam and Feather. I need to get back to Feather in the morning. I know what the

Holy Spirit has been telling me this year. I sense that my Lord and Savior Jesus Christ is placing an urgency upon the hearts of His believers.

I thank Mom for a wonderful supper and compliment the girls on being godly women. They accept the compliment but look at me as if they doubt my sincerity. Everyone probably thinks I'm crazy, but God's word—the Bible—gives me an urgency to tell the people I love how much they mean to me. I've wasted so much time.

I go to my room and open the Bible. It falls open to Luke 21, and I find these Scriptures to be ones I want to hold near my heart.

Luke 21:15. *For I will give you words and wisdom that none of your adversaries will be able to resist or contradict.*

Luke 21:28. *When these things begin to take place, stand up and lift up your heads, because your redemption is drawing near.*

I choose the Scriptures I want to share with Feather and Liam. Feather is receptive now, but Liam is hostile. I'll share with Feather first, and she can take back the message of salvation to her people, and then I'll take the message to Liam.

Step one: to hear. Romans 10:17. *Consequently, faith comes from hearing the message, and the message is heard through the word of Christ.*

Step two: to believe. Hebrews 11:6. *And without faith it is impossible to please God, because anyone who comes to Him must believe that He exists and that He rewards those who earnestly seek Him.*

Step three: to repent. Acts 17:30. *In the past God overlooked such ignorance, but now He commands all people everywhere to repent.*

Step four: to confess. Matthew 10: 32–33. *Whoever acknowledges Me before men, I will also acknowledge him before my Father in heaven. But whoever disowns Me before men, I will disown him before my Father in heaven.*

I knock on Dulcie's door. She and Alexa say in unison, "Come in." They are so close and so cute. I'm lucky to have them in my life.

I step inside, smiling, and I state, "You girls are so cute when you answer in unison. Have I ever told you that?"

"No," they say together and giggle, because they accidently did it again.

I sit on the edge of their bed and ask, "Dulcie, can I talk to you for a minute about salvation?"

"Of course, Coda. What do you want to know?" Dulcie asks, and Alexa quietly slips out the door, closing it behind her.

"Dulcie, I've been studying ever since our visit last spring. Thank you again for sharing with me where I was falling short. It would've been awful to have known God, believed Jesus was His son and that He came for my sins, and then just ended my learning there. I would've fallen short and not made it to heaven to live with Him. I have heard the word. I believe Jesus is God's Son. I have repented of my sins. I know I am unworthy of such a gift, but I must accept it. Christ gave His life willingly, so that I could be with Him in heaven. I have not confessed who He is to anyone until now, to you. I'm going to share this with a friend tomorrow. She is searching for the truth. I know I am to tell her. My question is, after my confession of faith and her confession, what should we do next? I love Him so much for what He has done for me, and I want to do more, if at all possible."

Dulcie writes something on a paper. "Here are the Scriptures that will lead you to the answer you want. I told you at the pond that you have to rely on God. He will reveal to you what you are to know when you are ready. You are ready. Always go to God in prayer and ask Him to reveal to you His truth from the Bible. He has told us that there'll be false prophets, and you need to know if what they say is the truth by weighing everything they say against the Bible. There'll be many fooled and swayed, because they're too trusting to double-check what they're being taught. Tell me how tomorrow goes, okay? Maybe you'll share who this friend is and bring her to the house. I would like to meet the girl that has impressed my little brother like this," Dulcie answers. She hands me the paper, on which she's written some Scriptures.

"Thanks, Dulcie. If I'm late tomorrow, will you cover for me?" I ask. "I'll explain to the folks when I get home."

"Sure, we'll at least know you're all right and not doing something stupid," she says. "I'll calm the folks, if they need it, but you'll be home on time."

Later, I wrote down what I wanted to share with Feather and Liam, and I knew which verse I'd choose for baptism.

Step five: to be baptized. Romans 6: 3–5. *Or don't you know that all of us who were baptized into Christ Jesus were baptized into His death? We were therefore buried with Him through baptism into death in order that, just as Christ was raised from the dead through the glory of the Father, we too may live a new life. If we have been united with Him like this in His death, we will certainly also be united with Him in His Resurrection.*

I look at my list. I need this so that when Feather's beauty again takes my breath away, I'll be able to sound intelligent. This is so important; I want to do my very best to explain it. God said that He would give me the words I needed when I needed them to confess His name. *I will hold you to that, Lord*, I pray silently. I read in my Bible until I fall asleep. It's the best rest I've had in a couple of years. The alarm rings, and I shut it off before it wakes my brothers. I slip out into the crisp air of early fall. My breath hangs on the air as I breathe deeply of the fresh country air, and I thank God for fresh air, clean water, and indoor bathrooms. I slip back into the house and resurface shortly and drive to the cave. I journey through the tunnels now as if I'd traveled them all of my life. I find Feather, kneeling in prayer on her blanket. *Lord, please give me the words, and help me to be the witness worthy of the message. Amen.*

"Hello, Feather," I say as I approach her. "I don't want to scare you again."

"Hello. I tethered my falcon outside. He is watching for breakfast—or lunch, depending on when he finds it. He'll begin to squawk when he sees it. I hope you rested well. I know I did. Just knowing that my journey has come to an end is a comfort," she says.

"Feather, as I studied the Bible, I was led by the Holy Spirit to understand God's plan for our salvation. That means Jesus is the only one that can save us. We can't save ourselves by being good or doing good works. We have only one thing to do, and that is to accept His gift of salvation," I say. "Do you know who Jesus is, Feather?"

"I believe there is only one true, living Great Spirit and that He has created everything that exists. He has told us to take care of the earth and all of its creatures," Feather says. "What is this gift you speak of, if it is not what we already have in the land, water, and air?"

"God sent his only Son as a sacrifice for us. Jesus died for our sins, and we have to accept His gift of dying in our place," I begin. "We're all sinners and fall short of being able to know God. Jesus made the ultimate sacrifice for us. He gave Himself because He was the only one pure enough to do this."

"We have heard of this Jesus, and we believe that this was the Great Spirit's way of making a divine, direct connection from the Great Spirit to earth," Feather answers. "That this Jesus was to be the expression of the

Great Spirit's love and great desire to connect with us. I believe that when we're not of one mind with the Great Spirit, we're at an imbalance, and what you call sin enters into people. We were created in perfect harmony, but it is the human side of us that causes us to be prideful and do the wrong actions and desires. We must refocus and accept our Great Spirit's divine connection that He has sent to save us. We must remember that we were created by the One who made everyone and everything to be good. We'll minister to our people to accept this connection and walk in the path that the Great Spirit has made for us."

I'm amazed at Feather's conviction. I didn't know much about her religion or knowledge of God. It sounds like God has provided a way to tell all of the people of the world of His plan. I go ahead and explain what I know, as I understand it. "Jesus loved us so much, He voluntarily came and gave His life that we might live. He felt pain, like any other man, but He chose to suffer and die for our sins. This is the *gift* that God provided, so that we might be forgiven of our sins. When we accept Jesus as our savior, God looks at us and sees His Son and doesn't see our sins. When Jesus was crucified for our sins, He died on the cross, but He rose from the dead three days later. He conquered the grave and lives with His Father in heaven. He will return to earth and destroy all who do not know Him. I believe the Great War your grandfather saw in his vision was Jesus, fighting that last battle. Old Testament prophets have predicted the end times, and the book of Revelation in the New Testament tells of those final days. Jesus will cleanse the earth, and then those of us who know Him will live with Him in heaven."

Feather comments, "Our prophets, as you call them, have told of the end times also. I have heard this story, but I thought it was just a legend. I must believe this?"

I say emphatically, "Yes, we've all sinned and cannot be with God as long as we're sinners. We cannot pay for our own sins or anyone else's; only Jesus Christ could pay for them. He could do this for us, because He is the only one who is blameless."

Feather paces and thinks and then says, "I understand purification. We have purification ceremonies, but are you telling me that we can't purify ourselves?"

I boldly reply, "That's right. Only accepting Jesus as the Son of God and the gift of salvation can make you pure enough to live with God."

Feather walks over to me and takes my hands and holds them, as if this physical connection will help her find the words to explain what she understands. "I want to be with the Great Spirit forever. I accept this divine connection of Jesus that He provided for me. I believe that when I'm right with the Great Spirit and repent, He sees my divine connection as a creation that is good, and He is well pleased. I believe I will be given the words and direction I need to lead my people to this salvation. Many have not fallen away and will help me, but for those who have lost their harmony, I will help them find it. Salvation is not a place or something we can personally sacrifice to achieve. It is the inner harmony of knowledge that the Great Spirit shall give us when we understand. You call it the Holy Spirit. He shall give us this understanding when we seek and accept it."

I squeeze her hands in confirmation that we are on the same page and understand this message in the same way. Smiling, I say, "That's right. Jesus told us that He'll be going ahead of us to prepare a place for us in heaven—that in heaven there are many mansions and beauty beyond comprehension. We'll feel no pain or sorrow. If we confess who He is to others, then He will tell God that He knows us. We have to first know Him, who He is, and what He has sacrificed for us and why. There is only one God, creator of everything. Your people need to follow five steps: 1) hear who Jesus is; 2) believe who He is; 3) repent and acknowledge that they've sinned; 4) confess who Jesus is to others; and 5) be baptized and raised in newness of life. I haven't done the final step myself yet."

"Tell me more of being baptized," Feather requests.

"It's when you make your confession of faith of who Jesus is, and you follow him into the grave," I begin, but Feather interrupts.

"I must die, then?" she asks, alarmed, dropping my hands and taking a step back.

I quickly try to do a better job of explaining. "Yes—well, not exactly. It's a symbol of a watery grave. You go under the water and then come up as a person cleansed of her sins. Jesus conquered death and arose from the grave to live eternally in heaven with God. You do this to symbolize the death and burial of the old you and arise as the new you, with Jesus living inside of you. If you really know who Jesus is, you will want to do this. In the New Testament, Jesus was baptized by John to give us an example of what we should do obediently. He had not died yet, and I'm sure that the crowds didn't understand the full meaning until He was gone. It was to symbolize the washing away of sins and rising to sin no more."

Feather paces and thinks again and then says, "Where I live and where my people live there is little water. There are no streams or lakes. What will I do?"

Now it's my turn to pace. After thinking for a while, I remember about a time that might help us, so I tell Feather, "My grandfather once baptized a man at the fellowship home. The man couldn't be moved. Grandfather said that the Greek word for baptism means to dip in liquid or to take liquid and put it on or over the person. I think you would use the last one, but I'll ask my dad."

Feather seems to be anxious and says, "When can I be baptized? I must get back to my people and tell them of the good news."

She has heard and believes. It's time for step three, so I ask her, "Are you ready to pray and accept this gift of salvation?"

"Yes, I'm ready, Coda the Messenger. Please lead me in this prayer. I know you know my heart to be true. I have already prayed for your guidance, and the Great Spirit has answered that prayer. He'll honor our sincere prayers now. I know He will," Feather says.

I take Feather's hand and lead her over to the fur rug on the floor. I say, "Let's kneel, bow our heads, and pray." We close our eyes, bow our heads, and I begin. "Dear Jesus, my Lord and Savior," I say, and Feather repeats the words in her own language. "Thank you for providing a way for my sins to be forgiven. I know I have sinned against God, and I accept your gift of salvation. I am so sorry, Jesus, that You had to suffer and die because of my sins. I know that I was on Your mind and heart as You endured Your crucifixion. They mocked and beat You. Those wounds should've been mine, but You did this for me because You love me. Forgive me now and accept my service as I tell others of Your love. Amen."

We both raise our heads and embrace. It is as though our arms already belong to Him. It doesn't feel like a normal hug. It feels like the welcoming embrace of a loved one who has come home after a very long time of being away.

CHAPTER 11

CONFESSION, COMMITMENT, & CONTENTMENT

I can't wait to get home. I finally can be totally and completely honest with my family. I don't know what they'll say or do, but it doesn't matter now. I feel as if a burden has been lifted, and my mind, body, and soul are at peace. It's true what they say—that the Holy Spirit will come to you and reside in you when you really know Jesus.

I can't wait for supper; this is when I'm going to share my news with my family. I shower and help Mom in the kitchen. The hunters come home early. We sit down at the table and say prayers of thanksgiving for the food, family, and health. This simple family tradition takes on more importance somehow. I think back to what the girls and Liam said about my not listening at the table to what everyone shares about their day or their hopes and dreams. The girls were right. I know I never listened before. I heard words with my ears but not with a caring heart. If it wasn't about me, I could not have cared less. Now, I can't wait to tell them my news of accepting Christ, but I also am drawn to take a more humble place in my family. I want to put them first and to listen to what's important to them. I listen quietly through supper to all of the sharing that goes on around our evening table. I feel their disappointment; I laugh and cry at their stories. I can't believe I've missed such richness all of this time. We gather together at supper every evening, but this is the first time I've thought of anyone but myself. This saddens me. When the meal is over, Dad notices I've been very quiet, so he asks if I'm all right. I smile and say, "I accepted

Jesus's gift of salvation today and asked His forgiveness for my sins. Now, I want to ask all of you to forgive me as well. I know I've been focused only on myself. I love all of you so much. Please forgive me."

Well, next comes laughing and crying and pats on the back, with "It's about time" speeches. We all go into the living room, and they ask me how it happened, or how I'd been led to this decision. Liam is gone from the group; I saw him slip off down the hall to our bedroom. I need him here so I can witness to him through my testimony. That thought may not have been my own; it's probably from the Holy Spirit. The old me would've only cared about me. Listening to the Holy Spirit is new to me. I feel so privileged that God cares enough to communicate with me. I make a pledge to always act on what is being placed upon my heart from the Spirit.

"Excuse me for a minute, you guys. I'll be right back," I say and slip off to get Liam, hoping he'll come.

As I enter the bedroom, I ask, "Hey, what's going on Liam?"

Liam avoids looking at me. He scans the room for a book or anything to occupy his hands. Finding nothing, he answers, "Nothing. I just wanted to relax."

I move close to him, place my hand on his shoulder, and say, "Liam, it would mean a lot to me if you would join us in the living room for a little while."

He squirms a bit but then strides out of the room, saying, "Sure, bro. Let's go."

I stop at the bathroom for a minute, so no one will know that I went after him. Then I return to the living room.

I say to the folks, "Please be patient with me. I've done something I wasn't supposed to do. I know I was wrong, but if you'll please wait until I finish, then I think you'll understand. I personally understand now, and I didn't when these things were happening to me."

"Okay, son, we'll be quiet until you are finished," Dad says.

I begin with meeting Feather, but I don't say where right away. I start all the way back at the beaver's dam, because apparently that was God's first push for me to connect with Feather. I tell of the first sighting of the falcon and his role in finding me for her. I tell them the whole story until finally, I tell them about Feather and our confession of faith. Dad starts to say something at the part about the cave, but Mom holds on tight to his arm. I sure am glad they sat together on the couch. I quickly finish my story, and I ask Dad if he would be the one to baptize both of us. He pauses, looks at Mom, and then swallows what I'm sure he wants to say about the cave. He ends up saying he would be honored. Dad studied to be a minister, and Grandpa did his ordination right before he died. Dad never sought a church to pastor, because he felt he would be able to witness to more people by working out among the crowds.

Dad asks, "When do you want to be baptized?"

I look hopefully at him and say, "I would like to be baptized at the pond tomorrow morning, if that's okay. Feather may want to join me."

"Sure, I think that'd be perfect. But you do realize the pond will be awfully cold this time of year," Dad says, smiling.

I think he is pleased with me. It feels so good to not be letting someone down. *I wonder if the Holy Spirit gives you common sense*, I think. And then I immediately tell myself, *No, I don't think so. I think you either have it or you don't. Maybe the Holy Spirit just helps a person to make better choices.*

I remember Feather's question about sprinkling or pouring water over someone instead of immersion. I ask, "Speaking of water, the temperature won't matter to us. If it is okay with you, Dad, Feather said they don't have much water where she is from and could they sprinkle or pour the water on the people?"

Dad takes a moment and picks up his study Bible from the end table beside him. After thumbing through a few pages, he answers, "Sure, they can sprinkle or pour the water. In the Greek translation, the word used could mean to sprinkle or to pour."

I'm relieved that I didn't tell Feather something that wasn't true, because it would only serve to confuse her. I want her to be certain of the message she is to tell others. I then say, "I'll go to the cave in the morning and talk to Feather. I'll come right back, if that is okay."

Dad states flatly, "No, it's not." My heart sinks, and I'm sure it shows on my face, but Dad smiles and continues. "I think we'll all go with you. We'll wait at the pond, and when you finish your talk with Feather, bring her with you. I'm sure everyone else would like to meet her."

"That'll be perfect," I say. "I know Feather is in a hurry, and her grandfather is to pick her up and take her home soon."

The next morning is crisp but warm for November. We all ride over to the pond in the old farm pickup. All of the kids ride in the back, and Dad and Mom in the front. We walk down to the pond together, and then only I go into the cave to get Feather. I make it over to Feather's cave in record time. The distance from my quarry cave and her mined one is probably over a half a mile, and it gives me time to settle my thoughts and prepare myself in prayer. I guess I should've offered to pick her up at her entrance, but I don't know where that is or even if I could drive to it. If it is on the edge of Southard's oldest property, I would have to go through the plant to reach it. I prefer this route; it seems perfect. I have the path memorized, which gives me the privilege of daydreaming about the next few days with Feather. I exit the last crack in the wall to enter the mine, and I find Feather packing her things. An older man is with her. I realize we will never have those days together, and it saddens me. I focus on today as I announce my presence. "Excuse me," I say. I feel a little uncomfortable about just barging in, but it's kind of hard to knock on stone walls.

"Coda, I'm so glad you came! This is my grandfather. Grandfather, this is the messenger, Coda," she says excitedly.

"I came to tell you that my dad is going to baptize me in the pond this morning. Would you like to join me?" I ask.

"Grandfather, it is what we asked of the Great Spirit," Feather says. Then she turns to me. "We prayed this morning, when Grandfather came to take me home, that the Great Spirit would provide a way for me to do this baptism. He's brought you and your father here in answer to our prayer. Is this the way baptisms are always performed, by the father?" Feather asks.

"No, fathers don't baptize just because they're fathers. My father comes from a long line of ministers. My great-grandfather, my grandfather, and my dad are all ordained ministers," I answer. Then I add, "Usually, the minister of your church is the one to baptize you, but anyone who has been baptized can baptize someone."

"I understand," Feather says.

A part of me is so excited about my decision to follow my Lord into the watery grave of baptism, but another part is very sad about Feather's departure. I wonder where she lives; maybe I could visit her. They are ready and looking at me, so I say, "My family is waiting for us at the pond. We should be going."

"Coda, I shared with Grandfather the truth that you have given me," Feather says on the walk through the cave.

"Sir, what do you think of what Feather has told you?" I ask, looking into the coal-black eyes of the man I know only as Grandfather.

"I think it is what we've been looking for, and I want to know more," he says.

I feel so protective of her. I offer all that I have to keep her safe, until we can meet again. "Feather, I want to give you my Bible. Always double-check what people are saying as the truth against God's word—even the things I say. Make sure you prove them through God's word. A very wise woman told me this once. If it cannot be proven by God's word, then don't believe it. False prophets will try to fool you, as well as men that change the words so that it fits what they want to do, not what God wants them to do."

"Thank you, Coda. I will read and study. I also believe that the Great Spirit knows my heart and will help me with the words I need to reach those who are lost. I see you have highlighted some of the teachings in your Bible. It will make me feel closer to you, just knowing that you read these same words," Feather answers. "What are the red letters?"

I answer wistfully, "Those are the actual words of Jesus speaking. The Bible is made up of the Old Testament, which was before Jesus came to earth, and the New Testament, which is after He was here. That is very simplistic, but maybe when you get home, you can find a church, and you can ask a minister the questions that are bound to come up over time. I wish I could be there to answer them."

I hope that what I've told her were God's words and not my own, because there is nothing more important than a person's salvation. I'd hate to have *not* told her something because I failed to prepare myself. I felt a peace, so I knew all was well. Maybe that's what she meant when she said the Great Spirit would give her the right words.

We stop a few times on the way through the cave. Some of the crevices are narrow, and the ceilings are low. Grandfather has the most difficulty. We climb down the rope ladder, make our way around the lower ledge, and climb up to the last ledge. Grandfather stops.

Feather grabs my shirt as I'm on my knees, ready to crawl through the last section. She asks, "What is wrong, Grandfather?"

His eyes glisten in the dim light as he speaks. "Do you see it, Feather? Do you see the symbolism? The Great Spirit is having us come out of the womb of Mother Earth to be born again."

Feather looks behind her, from where we had come, and then forward to the narrow tunnel. She smiles, hugs her grandfather, and says, "Grandfather, let's not waste another minute. I'm ready for this new life."

She nods for me to continue. We are all silent as we pass through the final passage, where we have to crawl. As we crawl out of the cave, my family is on the dam, watching for our return. I can't tell what they are thinking when I emerge from the hole in the earth, with two Indians, wearing full traditional dress, following me. It didn't seem odd at all to me, but I can tell by their expressions that they're more than a little shocked. I guess I'd forgotten to tell them that part when I related my journey in accepting Christ as my Savior. They probably think I went back in time and brought with me some time-travelers. I know that's what I thought the first time I saw Feather. The family remains at the top of the dam, and I do our introductions there.

Mom speaks first. "Feather, your dress and moccasins are beautiful. Can you get them wet and not ruin them?"

Feather stands straight as an arrow with her head held high as she answers, "Thank you for your compliment, but the most important thing to me right now is that I follow my Jesus into the watery baptism. I'm sure my clothes will be fine and that the Great Spirit would want me in my traditional dress to accept this gift. I can't wait to start my new life as my people's Faith Keeper."

I can tell Mom is impressed. Dad asks which one of us wants to go first. Feather steps up to me and says, "Coda, my messenger and guide, I would be honored if you would lead us into this last step of our salvation." Her eyes lock with mine and the light within her soul lights the golden flecks in those beautiful brown eyes. They seem to come to life, and I knew I could deny her nothing.

"I would be honored. Dad, I'll go first," is all I can say.

"Fine, Coda, you need to answer a few questions first. Who is Jesus Christ?" Dad asks.

I answer with confidence, "Jesus Christ is the Son of God."

"That's right. Coda, are you blameless?" Dad asks.

I feel so humbled as I answer this question. "No, I have sinned and asked Jesus to forgive me for my sins. I accept His gift of salvation."

"Follow me into the pond," Dad says.

We enter the pond, and it gets so deep so quickly that it doesn't take but a few steps before we're over our waist in the water. Dad places one of his hands behind my upper back. He raises his other hand to the heavens, and says, "I baptize you in the name of the Father, the Son, and the Holy Spirit." Then he braces my back, puts his hand on my forehead, and lays me down into the water. He pulls me up and out of the water. He gives me a brief hug and tells me he's proud of me, and we walk out of the water.

Feather is talking to her grandfather in their native language. We don't understand a word that they're saying. I walk over to Mom and the others and wrap up in a blanket she's brought. Feather turns to my dad and says, "I've been telling Grandfather, since his arrival this morning, all that I have learned. He has listened and believes as well. May he make a confession of faith to you?"

"Yes, of course. What is your grandfather's name?" Dad asks.

"He is called Sani. It means the 'old one,'" she says.

"Messenger's dad, let me look into your eyes," Sani says.

He faces off with Dad, and they look into each other's eyes for a full minute.

Sani says, "I see the eyes of my ancestors looking back at me. This is good. Granddaughter, you have chosen well. Coda is the one we have been seeking to guide us. Messenger's dad, do you have Indian brothers' blood in you?"

"Yes, my great-grandmother was Cherokee. Why?" Dad replies.

"This is good. I must be lead on this quest by the elder of the guardian. My vision said it would be a brother. We must begin. My granddaughter and I have many to save before the final war. All of the signs are in place, and my vision said it's time," Sani says. He takes Feather's hand, and they walk to the water's edge.

Feather turns to Dad and asks, "Can you pour or place the water upon us as a baptism? Where we live there is little or no water, and I would like to know how to do this."

"Sure, I can do that," Dad says. He goes to the pickup, gets the tire tool, and pries the bowl-shaped hubcap off the pickup. He returns to the pond and dips it into the water, washing it clean. Then he fills it with water and walks over to Feather and Sani. Dad asks them their confessions of faith. They respond one after another, each telling what they know in their own words. Feather asks if her grandfather might go first, and then Dad baptizes her also, by dipping his fingers into the bowl and sprinkling the water over their heads. They walk back to the dam. We pause only for a minute or two on the dam. Feather and I say our good-byes.

With my heart aching, I ask, "Will I see you again?"

"If the Father of Jesus thinks we should, I'm sure it will be so. Good-bye, Coda, my messenger and guide. Thank you," Feather answers, and I see tears in her eyes as well. She walks over to me, holding eye contact. She smiles and touches my cheek, and as I lean into her caress, she leans up and kisses the other cheek. "I'll miss you. Thank you for all you've done for us."

I call after their retreating backs, "Good-bye, and I hope that God will let our paths cross again. I'll pray for you and your people. Be safe, and good-bye, Sani." I try to sound like a wise leader, but I feel that I've been the one led, and I thank God that I have.

Sani waves a good-bye. They go back down the dam and into the cave opening. As I watch the last of her fringed moccasin disappear inside, I hear a call from the trees. I look up, and there's the falcon. He makes eye contact with me, and then he flies north. He'll be at the opposite side of the hill and the opening of the other cave when they come out, I'm sure. I'll miss him.

We all turn toward home, and Dad and I race to the pickup, because we are cold and wet. I think my nerves are making me shake as much as the cold. Mom and Dad and I ride in the front, and the rest of the kids are in the back. I notice Liam sitting apart from the others, ignoring what they're saying. I wonder if that is what Dulcie meant when she said that I was detached when I was in a group that was talking about God. I look out the window and think of how empty the sky will be without the falcon. I'd gotten used to watching for him in the evenings.

CHAPTER 12

SCRIPTURE, SECRETS, & SANI

Feather thumbs through the pages of Coda's Bible and turns to Revelation, because she remembers Coda talking about this book. Then she says softly, "Grandfather, do you believe we are coming to the end of time?"

"I believe that no one knows the 'when,' just that it's coming. I have a great desire to make sure as many of our friends and family know Jesus, as your friend has put it. They must get back to the essence of the original desire by the Great Spirit—to live in harmony and balance with all of that which was created. I felt an urgency to do something after my vision a couple of years ago. I just didn't know what it was that I should do, so we prayed, and our Great Spirit has answered us today. I believe it was that realignment that we were missing," Sani says.

They ride silently for a few miles before Sani says, "Read to me from the Bible. What did Coda find important? You said he underlined some of the words."

Feather places the Bible on her lap and lets it fall open, and then she begins to read aloud.

"Signs of the end of the age." Feather pauses briefly and says a silent prayer. *Great Spirit, show us what we need to know. Continue to guide us safely to You.* Then she continues. "This is in Luke, chapter twenty-one, verses five through seven. *Some of his disciples were remarking about how the temple was adorned with beautiful stones and with gifts dedicated to God. But Jesus said, 'As for what you see here, the time will come when not one stone will be left on another; every one of them will be thrown down.' 'Teacher,' they asked, 'when will these things happen? And what will be the sign that they are about to take place?'"* Feather pauses to think and then says, "Coda told me these disciples were the men who walked this earth with God's Son. They knew him well and wrote these books in the New Testament to record what they saw and what they were taught."

"What does it say, Feather? Go on," Sani says as he watches the road and listens solemnly.

"These letters are in red, Grandfather, which means that it is Jesus talking," Feather says before continuing to read. "This is still in Luke 21, starting with verse eight. *He replied: 'Watch out that you are not deceived. For many will come in my name, claiming, "I am he," and "The time is near." Do not follow them. When you hear of wars and revolutions, do not be frightened. These things must happen first, but the end will not come right away.' Then he said to them: 'Nation will rise against nation, and kingdom against kingdom. There will be great earthquakes, famines, and pestilences in various places, and fearful events and great signs from heaven.'"*

"Feather, this is what the great shaking of the earth was like in my vision. There will be many wars, good against evil. I saw our people being tracked down like dogs. They were rounded up and put in cages. These things are happening now. Look at the wars in the news around the world. The earthquakes are stronger, the countries on every continent are having famine and pestilence. How do we prepare? What do we do next?" Sani asks urgently.

Feather can't believe that this book, the Bible, has been here all along and has wisdom in it for them to live by.

She looks back at the Bible and reads, *"But before all this, they will lay hands on you and persecute you. They will deliver you to synagogues and prisons, and you will be brought before kings and governors, and all on account of my name. This will result in your being witnesses to them. But make up your mind not to worry beforehand how you will defend yourselves. For I will give you words and wisdom that none of your adversaries will be able to resist or contradict. You will be betrayed even by parents, brothers, relatives, and friends, and they will put some of you to death All men will hate you because of me. But not a hair of your head will perish. By standing firm you will gain life.'"* Feather closes the Bible and lays it on the seat. She crosses her arms and looks out the window.

"What is wrong with you?" Sani asks.

"How can we ever understand what all these words mean? They say things to scare us and then hide what to do in words we don't understand! Can I trust Coda? It says right here that I will be betrayed by friends. My own father would just as soon sell me as not—I know this for certain," Feather says as she sulks. "I shall never have a normal life—one filled with family and many friends. Don't misunderstand, Grandfather. I love you dearly, and I am so grateful I have you in my life." Feather thinks back to the cave and Coda's face. She misses him so much already.

"Feather, you are upset because you do not understand right away. You like things to be easy and simple. Things worth knowing and putting in your heart are not this way. You must work at understanding. You must find answers. Call Coda," Sani says.

Feather looks out the window to conceal the tears in her eyes. She wants to talk to Coda, to see Coda again, but she knows they will probably never meet. She left him a note, but she wonders if he will ever return to the cave and find the clues she left for him. Even if Coda does find the message left behind, she and Grandfather will be so very far away. And they may have to move yet again before school is out. *No, it will be best if Coda doesn't try to find me*, she thinks. *He will be safer this way. I mustn't give in and contact him.* Then, barely audible, she says, "I can't . . . he will be safer if I don't ever talk to him again."

Sani knows he should change the subject and that what she says is true. He is worried that it won't be long before they will have to move again. But he will move a hundred more times if it keeps his precious granddaughter safe. He says, "I think we should stop for lunch, and I need some gas. Watch for someplace where you want to eat." He pulls into the Sinclair station in Fairview and fills the gas tank.

"I've decided on Taco Mayo," Feather says as Sani gets back into the car. "We can drive through and not even get out of the car. I'm starved. How about a dozen tacos?" Feather asks, smiling for the first time since they left the cave. She knows her grandfather loves her and can't help the evil that stalks them.

"Sounds perfect, but you know I'll have tacos all over me. How about we get the tacos and find a place to have a picnic?" Sani asks as a compromise, seeing Feather's fearful agitation. He knows she is afraid that the men at Southard will soon be following them. He and Feather had always kept the iron gate locked so that no one would know they were inside. Somehow, these men discovered them and waited for them to come out. The men were unaware of another exit.

"Grandfather, how can you be sure that no one followed us?" Feather adds as she scans the area, as she always does when she's in a town. The old survival instincts kick in, and she watches for anyone who resembles him. When he gets this close, she knows it is only a matter of time before she will see him. Fortunately, the last several times, she saw him before he saw her. Feather bows her head and prays. *Great Spirit, give me eyes as sharp as a falcon, and make me alert to the danger that seeks me. Please keep Grandfather safe. He is getting old, and I know he would do anything for me, but don't let him give his life to save mine.*

Sani sees her in prayer, and his heart goes out to her. He battled this evil man before and came away bloody and beaten, but he has kept Feather safe. He would gladly do it again and again, but he has to be honest with himself. He is getting older. He reaches across the seat to hold her hand and says, "We left by the back entrance. No one was even near our car. We watched from the rearview mirrors, and no one followed us. We would have seen them by now. And no, I do not think that it was your father. He does not know where to look for you, so relax. I'm sure it was someone from the gypsum plant or an officer of the law that we heard at the cave entrance. We hurt no one, nor any of their land. Don't worry, my little bird."

CHAPTER 13

MISERY, MYSTERY, & MOUNTAINS

The old radio in the pickup plays the Hank Williams song "I'm So Lonesome I Could Cry." It just seems to punctuate the way I feel. I've felt such a loss since Thanksgiving. The school year has flown by, and things are going smoothly everywhere except in my head and heart. I try to witness to Liam, and he blows me off like I'm an annoying gnat. Now, he avoids me like the plague.

Dulcie enters the kitchen door, stomps the snow from her boots, and begins to peel off the layers of winter clothing. "I can't believe how long it took me to get home from class tonight. Those roads are dangerous. I thought it was spring break. This last snowstorm is bad. Has Rodney called?"

Mom gives her a hug. "I'm proud of your dedication. There are not many girls who would take the extra classes in the afternoon and evening of their senior year. I miss you, though." Then Mom adds, "Yes, Rodney called and said that the train would be coming through Southard tomorrow. He would be able to see you while they take on a load of sheetrock. He'll call later with the time."

Dulcie asks, "Alexa home yet?"

"Nope, she's with a group of juniors, planning college-bound things this evening," Eli says. He's working on routing the television wires into

100

the den. A lady at church bought a new television and gave the family her old one.

"Braden isn't coming home this week," Fuller says sadly, returning to cleaning up the files on Mom's computer. "Braden comes home less and less now that he shares an apartment with Colton, and the rigs are so far away. I miss him."

"Mom, I'm going to take a walk over to the pond and back for some exercise," I say. "I'm getting cabin fever, and we've only been out of school half a day."

"Okay, but take a coat," Mom says, and then she smiles because she knows she doesn't need to tell me to put on a coat anymore.

I step out, buttoning my jacket. I start off walking and then try to jog but soon find that the snow is too deep. I finally reach the pond. Maybe it's not the pond but the cave I want to see. I miss Feather immensely, and there hasn't been a day that goes by that I don't kick myself for not finding out her full name, or where she lives, or at least her phone number. She has my name in my Bible and a detailed map of where I live, so she could've gotten in touch with me. Maybe she doesn't want further contact. She's probably busy finishing her senior year.

Maybe I'll check the cave, I think. *Feather and Sani might have forgotten something, and I'll need to find her to give it back.* With a flashlight in my pocket, I walk to the cave. It isn't long before I'm at Feather's cave—I'd come to think of it as hers. It's dark, quiet, and cool, with no campfire and no firefly eyes to warm it. I round the center pillar and let my flashlight beam sweep the room. I see Feather's small clay pot—the one she said was a family heirloom. It is tucked behind a rock and only visible as I come out of the crack in the wall. She will definitely want me to return it. If I seriously search for her now, it would be considerate. I couldn't be thought of as a stalker. She has no idea how often I think of her. I'd avoided doing a search for her on the Internet, but now, Google here I come. I have a very good reason to stalk her—I mean, look for her. I just hope I know enough about her to find her. I'll try the social networks first, since I know only her first name. I wonder if I can Google just "Feather" and get any hits for people? I guess I'll find out.

As I pick up the bowl, I see a note tucked inside—and it looks like it was written in a hurry.

Messenger, I hope you find this.

We can hear my falcon crying out his warning of danger. There were voices at the opening of the cave upon our return from the pond. We'll leave by your cave opening and walk aboveground to the car. I'll leave you a note along the way out. I would very much like to see you again.

Your friend,

Feather

How strange, I think. *Why were they afraid to go out this opening? Why was someone waiting outside? Was it a stranger? Was it the police?*

It's against the law to enter the caves on United States Gypsum's property, so maybe the cave isn't on our land. I don't hear anything, so I decide to look for the other opening. I was always curious where it might be. I find it—and there's a locked iron gate across the opening. Whoever was here must have locked it so that no one could enter again. The gate looks old and rusted; I think it has been here all along. As I'm about to leave, I notice that the lock is on the inside, and it looks newer than the gate itself. I step to the opening to look at the lock. Whoever was waiting for them to come out must have believed that they had no other way out. I'll ask Dad if he can find out if anyone was run off of Southard's property. Then the hair on the back of my neck stands straight up. I turn around and scan the room once more. I can't explain it, but I feel like someone or something is watching me. I scan the area outside the gate but see no one there . . . and then I notice a hunter's camera mounted on a tree, pointed directly at the cave opening. What an odd direction to point the camera. Deer aren't likely to take refuge in a cave, nor are turkeys. As hunters, we would have the camera take pictures of known paths to water. As I look at it, I feel like someone is looking back at me. I instinctively back into the shadows.

I'm in deep thought as I make my way back to my quarry cave. I listen for any unusual sounds. I go slowly and examine every possible place to put a note. Since I found the bowl and note, I know that whoever was outside and locked the opening doesn't know about the other opening, or that would've been blocked too. I crawl through the last portion of the cave, and then I look up and see a paper wedged in a crack. I think to myself, *Good job, Feather. Anyone crawling through here would be looking down, not up.* I crawl out and cautiously look around this time. I expect to see the falcon, but there isn't any wildlife—not a single bird, not even a rabbit. That fact isn't normal. I go quite a distance downstream and find a small fat cedar. I work and work at it until I dislodge it from its rocky soil. The roots are shallow because of the layer of gypsum. I carry it back to the cave, all the while watching the canyon rim. I still have the feeling I'm being watched. I place the tree in front of the opening and prop it up with rocks, and then I fluff snow around the base. I see I've left tracks going down the stream but not where I'd stopped to crawl into the cave. I don't know why, but I want to protect the cave—it's important to me that no one finds it. I feel like no one should know that I was here. I see another camera that a hunter has set up on the canyon's rim. It overlooks the ravine floor; maybe that was what was making me feel uneasy.

I walk home, wondering how many people know of the cave, and all I can think of is the family. I don't know which hunter has put out the camera, but the cave entrance isn't visible from the angle of the camera, so perhaps this hunter is unaware of its existence. It's on our land, and there's no reason for anyone else to be there without our permission. We have it posted everywhere: No Public Hunting. I go home and go straight to my room before opening the paper I'd found in the crack. It reads:

Messenger, I need to talk to you and explain something about my past, something about my family. I must see you. If I don't see you today, then Grandfather and I got away, and we'll be unable to make contact for a while. I can't take the chance of this note falling into the wrong hands. I hope to see you in May for my graduation. Find me, my friend. I need you. I wrote you a poem to help you.

North sixty-four past the Cherokee Indian door,
Follow the falcon to the west and stop at the eagle's nest.
Enchanted I shall be, when south you come and visit me.
Fisherman we will be when east down the lane you see,
Twenty-three, twenty-three, hide-and-seek, come find me.

Messenger, Messenger, don't tarry long,
And for you I shall play another song.
Your escort is waiting from before,
He shall guide you to my door.

FF

"What in the world is she talking about?" I ask aloud. "Indians, birds, fish—maybe it has to do with nature. How in blazes am I to find her from this poem, or is it a riddle?"

"Who? And what riddle?" Eli asks. "I love riddles."

I jump and whirl around, saying, "I didn't know you were there."

"I came in, and you were so absorbed in that paper, so I kept quiet," Eli answers.

"It must be some sort of coded message," I say, as much to myself as to Eli. I'm deep in thought, wondering about what she thinks she needs to explain. Who was it that might've found the message? Why would she be fearful if they did? Maybe she kept her name from me on purpose. Could she be in trouble?

"Fuller and Eli, come here for a minute," I call out, staring at the paper.

"I'm right here," Fuller says directly behind me, making me jump again, and I see that Eli never left.

"You sure are jumpy today. What's wrong with you?" Eli asks.

I fill them in quickly on where I'd been and what I'd found and about the cameras. "I can't explain it, but I'm afraid she's in trouble. You two are the smartest guys I know. If anyone can figure out this riddle, you can.

Here—sit down and see if you can figure out what she is talking about," I say.

They scour each word of the page, making notes.

"North sixty-four could be a highway number or an address," Fuller says.

"I think it's a highway number since it's the first line," I say. "And she adds the direction of north."

"That would make sense, because there are more directions given as well—west, south, and east. She is telling you how to get to her," Eli says, smiling.

"Let's get a map. If she's giving us directions, we know the starting point is Canton or Southard, Oklahoma, where we live," Fuller says as he turns to Oklahoma in the road atlas.

"I think you're right," I say, taking my finger and traveling slowly north, "Fairview, Orienta, Carmen . . . and *Cherokee*! What did it say about Cherokee?"

"North sixty-four past the Cherokee Indian door," Fuller reads. "Keep going a little farther past Cherokee."

"That's it! Just north of Cherokee is Highway 64, and it runs east and west. Read the next line," I say excitedly.

"Follow the falcon to the west, and stop at the eagle's nest," Fuller reads.

I take my finger and follow Highway 64, but I see nothing. "Do you guys see anything that matches the clue? I'm sure 'falcon' means Falcon Feather and that we are to go west on 64 to find her, but there's nothing!" I complain. "Highway 64 extends all the way to the end of the Oklahoma panhandle."

Eli states, "Wait, 64 doesn't end with the Oklahoma border. What state is next to the panhandle?"

"New Mexico," Fuller says, immediately flipping the pages of the atlas to New Mexico.

"Find out where the highway goes and follow it. We all just assumed she lived in Oklahoma," Eli says.

"The highway dips down to Clayton, up to Capulin . . . Raton . . . and back down to Cimarron, and then over to . . . Eagle Nest. We found it!" Eli says, grabbing me and dancing a little jig.

"It says to stop at the eagle's nest—at Eagle Nest. Well, we can't very well knock on every door in an entire town, looking for someone. Let's pull up the Internet maps. Fuller, type in Eagle Nest, New Mexico, and turn on the bird's-eye view. There's Eagle Nest; now zoom in closer. Highway 64 is known as Enchanted Circle Scenic Byway! I can't believe it. She's taking us right to her front door," I happily announce.

"'Enchanted I shall be, when south you come and visit me.' That's the next line, so we must go south on the Enchanted Circle loop," Fuller says, studying the map. To the south, the road curves, and then there is a turn to a housing subdivision. "The name of the road is Fisherman's Lane!" Fuller exclaims. "It worked! What's the next line?"

Eli reads, "Twenty-three, twenty-three, hide-and-seek, come find me."

"Well, it doesn't look like there are twenty-three houses so maybe it's an address," Fuller says as he types something into the computer. "There isn't a house at that address, but this is an old satellite view. A house could be there now."

"Well, if I get that close, I'll be able to see her falcon and find her, because the next line says my escort will guide me to her door," I say excitedly.

"What is our next move?" Eli and Fuller ask at the same time.

"How much money do you two have saved up?" I ask excitedly. "Who's up for a road trip?"

CHAPTER 14

ROAD TRIP, RIDDLES, & RESCUES

"I feel I need to go before graduation in May because she sounds troubled in this note. My gut feeling tells me to go immediately, that she needs us. Maybe it's the Holy Spirit. It led me to her once before. It says not to tarry, so I've got to talk Mom and Dad into letting me drive out there," I say, looking pleadingly at my brothers. "We have eight days left of spring break. Eight hours out and back takes care of one day. Seven days will surely be long enough to sort things out and help Feather. What do you guys think?"

Eli and Fuller look at each other, smile, and say, "We're in! I'll go raid my shoebox. I'll go find my stash." They head out in opposite directions, and I head for the living room, where Mom and Dad are watching television.

I fill the folks in on everything. I show them the note and tell them I feel like something is wrong. At first, I just thought I was missing Feather, but maybe it was the Holy Spirit trying to send me on my way. We discuss how far it is and that I've never been away without the family before. I remind them that I'll soon be eighteen, Eli is a couple of months from being sixteen, and Fuller is fourteen going on forty. They laugh and then talk it over, and then they insist that we take Dad's newer Dodge truck. It's a four-door with four-wheel drive, which will help if the snow gets worse. I thank my folks—I'm sure they know this means the world to me—and I run to the bedroom to tell the guys. They're almost finished packing when

I walk in the room. I throw some things in my duffel and run out to check the oil and tires on the Dodge. I put in an extra can of oil, tools, hazard light, and a jug of water. I throw in all three of our insulated coveralls, just in case we have to walk if the Dodge has trouble. I run back inside. Eli and Fuller sail by me out the door, heading to the truck with duffels stuffed and their arms loaded with something in big trash bags. I grab my duffel bag from the bedroom and run back through the house. I'm at the door to exit just as Liam comes through the door. I'd forgotten all about him. I feel awful. He's right; we treat him like he doesn't exist sometimes.

"What's going on? You guys taking a road trip in this weather?" Liam asks, smiling at me. I guess he notices my shocked look and realizes we hadn't thought about taking him.

"Yeah, I thought you were spending the night with your friends. I'm glad you're here. Do you want to go with us?" I ask, trying to sound as if nothing is wrong. He knows we hadn't given him a single thought. Mom fills him in on Feather's note and tells Liam that I'm going to see her. She never mentions where we're going or that the note was found in the cave, which I think is extremely important. But I don't tell him either. The thought that all of us are beginning to distrust Liam crosses my mind and makes me a little ill.

"Nah, I've got big plans for the break with my friends. You go on. I don't want to be cooped up with you guys in that old farm truck," Liam says, sauntering past us, ignoring Mom's presence as he steps around her. I know he is hurt to have been forgotten, because I would've been.

"We're taking the Dodge. Do you want to go now?" I ask hopefully, beginning to see the opportunity this might be to get closer to my brother.

"The Dodge?" Liam says, glaring at me. He turns to Dad, complaining, "I was going to ask to borrow the truck, Dad. That's not fair."

Dad puts his hand up before Liam starts to explode. "It's my decision, and the boys are taking the truck. You can use the farm pickup. It has been good enough for everyone except you. I think it's time you took your turn driving it instead of my truck. No arguing."

"Come with us, Liam," I call as he stomps away. "It'll be a trip for just the boys—minus Braden, of course."

"No!" Liam shouts and slams the bedroom door. I know he's mad, but I really feel like he's hurt, too, that we thought so little of him that we didn't invite him in the first place.

"You better be on your way, son. Don't worry about him. This will give me a chance to talk to him. He'll have to take me to work and come and get me," Dad says, smiling, like he'd planned it this way all along.

I kiss Mom on the cheek. She puts something in my pocket, and I'm out the door.

The guys are in the front seat, sitting like two bird dogs on point. Their noses point straight ahead, as if they've found their bird. I look down the south driveway, following their gaze, and see a dark-blue older model Malibu slip-sliding up the drive. I don't recognize the driver, but it's approaching dusk and getting harder to see. Before the car gets any closer, I take off down the north drive. Something tells me to leave quickly. We have a large U-shaped drive that goes around a small field. The south drive arrives at the front of the trailer, and the north is the other end of the trailer where the carport sits by the house. I leave by one way as the stranger arrives by another. Panic comes over me, making me feel sick. It's like last year, when I'd wake from dreams drawing me to the cave that left me confused and scared about the unknown. But like last year, I can't do a thing about it except give in to the overwhelming desire drawing me closer. I now wonder if it is Feather who draws me to her. I reach in my pocket, and as I feel Feather's notes, I breathe easier.

"Fuller, did you turn off the computer?" I ask, almost afraid of his answer. Liam's behavior and the stranger's arrival make me uneasy. I feel like I did when I covered the cave entrance—it's like I'm protecting something.

"Sure, why do you ask?" Fuller responds.

"I can't put my finger on it, but I think Feather is in danger, and that strange car has something to do with it. Doesn't it seem strange to you guys that shortly after I'm filmed on a stranger's camera that points straight at Feather's cave, that we would have strangers at our door. And they come in a freak spring snowstorm? What is so important that a person gets out in this weather? If they'd just wait a week, the weather will be clear. I don't want anyone to see what we were looking at on the map on the computer. You did bring along the road atlas, didn't you?" I ask nervously as I watch the rearview mirror, expecting to see car's lights following us.

"Did you bring Feather's notes?" Eli asks, panicked now.

"Yes, I have them. Get the map out and plot our course, navigators," I say, trying to lighten the mood. "I'm sure it's just the mystery of it all that's making me jumpy, and when I was at the cave, I felt like someone was watching me."

"Well, we left our written notes about the riddle out on the desk. Maybe it won't make any sense to anyone," Eli says, leaving unsaid what we all are thinking—that Liam will be the one to see them.

None of us wants to make any unnecessary stops, so we drive until our bladders can't take it any longer—all of twelve miles. In Fairview, we take care of business, top off the gas tank, and get three sixty-four-ounce Mountain Dews. After stopping within the hour along the roadside and then at Cherokee to take care of business again—large drinks have to go somewhere—I think that at this rate, we'll never reach New Mexico. We get to Highway 64 and hang a left, and then I set the cruise control. I think about Liam and wish he would've come with us. The guys are singing at the top of their lungs, bouncing off of the walls from all the caffeine in the Mountain Dew. I'm preoccupied by what could be Feather's family secret—something she has to tell me in person. She knows how difficult it would be to get to her, which scares me even more. I know that she wouldn't ask this of me if it wasn't important.

Rolling the window down, I complain, "Whose bright idea was it to bring along bean dip and chips?" Both of their hands go up as they stuff their faces and pass gas out of both ends. "Cut it out, will ya? I'm going to put you in the back—I mean it."

Eli proudly announces the obvious. "Sure, you will. There's two of us and one of you. Don't threaten us."

What was I thinking, bringing these two monkeys along? It seemed like a good idea at the time. I sneak a glance sideways at them. They're punching at each other over who got bean dip on Dad's seat. I smile and think about a couple of years ago, when Braden probably just wanted some peace and quiet so he could think, and I wanted to explore a beaver's dam. Life is funny.

I remember that Mom put something in my pocket, so I pull it out. It's a fifty-dollar bill. I figure it's her birthday money from Grandma; we will use it only in an emergency. I hope to be able to take it back to her.

"Guys, how much money did you come up with?" I ask. "We'll need to pace ourselves if we want it to last all week. Let's make this trip a vacation. What do you say?"

"Sure, I found seventy-three dollars and a roll of quarters, so eighty-three dollars," Eli answers.

"I came up with a hundred and thirty-seven. Mom slipped me a fifty, but I'd like to not use it if we don't have to, because I think it's from her birthday card that Grandma sent her. Dad gave me his credit card for emergencies and gas," I say.

Fuller doesn't say a word; he just looks out the window. We all know he's a little miser. He's always getting money for something and squirreling it away. If we get to go to a ball game, Dad gives us three dollars for snacks. Fuller never buys anything; he just accepts drinks or bites from the rest of us and pockets the three dollars. Eli is punching him to speak up. Finally, Fuller answers very quietly, "I lack two dollars from having four hundred."

"Okay, one of you pinheads figure how much we have altogether," I say, and before I get it out of my mouth, Fuller answers.

"Six hundred and seventy dollars—that's counting Mom's fifty, of course."

Sometimes I think that head of his is a calculator.

"Now divide that by seven and—"

"Roughly ninety-five dollars a day," Fuller says before I can finish. "Or a little over thirty-one dollars apiece to buy food and drinks, but we'll need to sleep in the truck because there isn't enough for a motel room."

"Good, thanks. We can make a plan now," I say, not having the slightest clue how far thirty-one dollars a day will take us. The thought of sleeping together in the truck could be an adventure. I just wish I'd thought of this earlier, and I'd have put the sleeping bags in the truck.

Then, as if Eli was reading my mind, he says, "It's a good thing I put sleeping bags in the tool box. We might want to sleep out in the mountains. Will we be close enough to see the mountains, Coda?"

"Yes, we'll be able to see the mountains. I'm so glad you guys are along. I don't think I'd have gotten very far without you," I say sincerely, thinking about my impulsiveness.

CHAPTER 15

CLUES, CABINS, & CAUGHT

We arrive at Eagle Nest right before dawn. We pull into a set of cabins just south of where Feather's clues stop. I figure Dad wouldn't mind buying us one night's lodging. The owners let us stay in their cheapest cabin. It's small, with two twin beds and a couch. I sleep for a couple of hours because I'm the only one with a driver's license. The others slept on the way here. Now I really wish Liam would've come along. He's sixteen and could've helped to drive.

When I wake, I'm alone in the cabin. I see my brothers lounging in chairs outside, looking at the lake. I go outside to join them, and I hear a familiar call from the air. I look up and see a falcon leaving the top of the tree. He circles a couple of times.

I smile and say, "Our guide is here. Let's go."

We load up into the Dodge, and I tell the boys to keep an eye on the falcon. He flies straight east and lands on a large, light-colored house. It has a wooden privacy fence all the way around it, including the large drive. On the gate is a sign that reads *23 Fisherman's Lane*. Fuller jumps out and opens the gate, and we pull through. I get out, walk up to the door of the house, and knock. I hear footsteps, but I can't see in—all the shades are drawn tight. Then I hear deadbolts and locked tumblers clicking. The door swings open, and Feather looks out furtively. Then she calls to the boys and me, "Quickly, inside please."

112

Once we're inside, she turns to me, and I see that tears have extinguished the light in her beautiful firefly eyes. She walks into my arms, and we stand there for what seems like a very long time. I rest my cheek on the top of her head and gently rock from side to side. It feels so right to hold her, but her soft sobs break my heart. When her crying subsides, I pull her away from me and gaze into her eyes looking for answers. It has occurred to me that Grandfather isn't here. Could he have had an accident?

I ask her, "What's wrong? Where's Grandfather?"

"Grandfather is gone, and I'm alone. Coda, I have deceived you. I'm sorry. Can you ever forgive me?"

"Feather, talk to me. I came as soon as my brothers and I figured out your riddle. I didn't go back to the cave until yesterday afternoon, so we found your note less than twenty-four hours ago. Why were you so cryptic? Why didn't you call me? You knew my phone number," I ask, studying her tear-stained face.

She makes sure all the locks on the door are in place and then leads us into another room. It's larger but has no windows and only one small light in the corner by a table.

"Sit, and I'll try to explain. Thank you to all of you for coming. I'm too afraid to use the phone, for fear they'll discover me. I don't know what I would've done if you hadn't come, because I believe they're close," Feather says sadly. "I can always tell. I've even stopped going to class this semester. I never enrolled anywhere after Thanksgiving."

"Who are 'they'? And where is your grandfather?" I ask again.

"It's my father and whoever is with him. He always has someone along. Let me begin at the beginning. My name is Charlotte Hilton. My parents separated when I was five—or so I believed. I remember my parents' fighting and arguing, usually ending the next morning with my mother having cuts and bruises. My mother would put me to bed before my father came home from work, and I wasn't allowed to come out of my room for any reason. I remember once I didn't mind her, and she spanked me so hard, I cried and cried. She held me and cried along with me, stressing that I had to learn to obey. I realize now she was protecting me the only way she knew how. Then my mother went away one night after one of their fights.

"My dad grabbed some clothes and took me away. We lived in one city after another. The one survival lesson my mom taught me was to stay quiet and out of my dad's sight. Finally, I guess he had to settle down and get a job and stay in one place for a while. I was eight, and some neighbor ladies said they'd take me to school. They asked my name, and before he could answer, I told them. Dad enrolled me, using my real name. Grandfather is my mother's father; he gave me my traditional name of Falcon Feather. He'd never stopped looking for me. He found me when I enrolled in school. Grandfather has many friends, and they were watching the school enrollments for a girl my age. Grandfather came to the schoolyard, and I knew him right away, and I ran to him. I wasn't happy with my dad. He was mean and hit me often. Grandfather asked if I wanted to live with him, and I ran from the schoolyard that day, and I haven't looked back since.

"Grandfather has always been good to me. He protects me and has taught me everything I know. He is a college graduate but prefers his traditional life. I do, too; it has kept us hidden and safe all these years. When we have to blend in, we can, but recently I've seen my dad, and I know he's coming close to finding me. Grandfather asked questions about him and found that he has a gambling debt and is in need of lots of cash to some loan sharks. During the last beating Dad gave me before I ran away with Grandfather, Dad was saying that he would have to only bruise my back from now on, because the men wouldn't pay for a bruised little girl. I didn't know what he meant then, but I'm pretty sure I do now. Coda, I'm scared. I know he's near. I'll be eighteen next month, and when I reach eighteen, I'm going to the authorities to tell them all that I know about my dad. Legally, they can't make me go home with him, and if they don't arrest him, I'll just disappear again. I'd hoped to one day be able to live among others without always searching the faces in a crowd for my nightmare to return. I've lied to you, and in so doing, I may have put you and your family at risk. I'm sorry. I've never been able to have close friends for fear my dad would find me through them. I had to take a chance and leave you and your family a note. I had to confide in someone. After finding my strength in God, I felt I didn't need to be fearful any longer and his confidence would be all I'd ever need." When Feather finishes speaking, she hangs her head in shame.

I ask, becoming more frightened about the answer, "Where's Grandfather now, Feather?"

Feather paces like she did in the cave. She must do this when she is worried. She looks up as a tear rolls off her cheek and says, "I don't know. He dropped me off and continued on to Utah when we returned at Thanksgiving. That's where we live. He took my cousin with him. She looks a lot like me, and he made sure to stop and talk to lots of people along the way. He's hoping to lead my dad away from me. It has worked before. But if my dad finds Grandfather and not me, he may take his anger out on Grandfather, knowing he has tricked him again. This place belongs to a friend of his from college. The man is one of only a few that my grandfather would trust with his life—or mine. I'm the only one here, and there is plenty of food, so I don't even have to go outside. The building looks like its empty at this time of year."

"Let's call the police," Eli says.

"No, we can't," Feather pleads as she wipes her eyes. "They'll arrest Grandfather for kidnapping and put him in jail. My father will gain custody of me and then will sell me before the courts ever sort the whole mess out. I just can't take the chance. Running is the only answer until I turn eighteen. After that, I can face my dad and swear Grandfather had nothing to do with my leaving my father."

I stop her and say, "We need to get that truck out of the drive. Is there a garage? Someplace we can hide our vehicle until we sort out what we can do to help you? If I'm right, I think your dad has traced your movement to Oklahoma. A strange car pulled into our driveway just as we were leaving. I think someone was watching me at the cave, and I felt an overwhelming need to get away from the house—and fast. We drove straight through to here last night."

"Coda, if this is true, I'm not safe here anymore. Did you leave any clue as to how you found me?" Feather runs from window to window, peeking out. "Do you think they followed you last night? They could be outside."

"I have your notes in my pocket, and we turned off the computer where we had searched out your clues," I say.

"The notes . . . we forgot about the notes we made to figure out the riddle," Fuller says, his voice full of emotion. "They're on the bedroom desk."

"Is there a phone here?" I want to help calm her down, but I have to have a plan. I say, "We may be alarmed over nothing. We can call home and see who the visitors were and what they wanted. It might not have been your dad."

"I pray not, because if it's him, he must be desperate. I mean only one thing to him: money. Besides that, he might harm your family," Feather says. Worry clouds her beautiful face and scares me.

When I call home, I get a busy signal. After an hour of busy signals, I call the telephone company's local office, and James, their field worker, answers the phone. He tells me the office girl has gone to the bathroom and will be right back. I ask him to please check the phone now, that it's an emergency. He tells me the phone seems to be off the hook. I tell him about not being able to get through; I'm out of town and I'm worried. One of the advantages of living in a small community is that everyone is your friend. James says he'll run by the house. I give him a few minutes to get there and then call the house again. He answers the phone.

"James, what did you find?" I ask.

"I found your folks beaten pretty badly. I called for an ambulance, so they've been taken to the hospital. They'll be all right, I'm sure. The robbers ripped the phone lines from the walls. Stole the guns and rifled through things looking for money, I guess, but Coda, are your brothers and sisters with you? We can't find them." James hesitates for a moment, and I can hear voices in the background. Then he says, "Wait a minute—the officer says that your folks said the girls slipped out the back door when the trouble began. The deputy found them hiding in the cellar, but the men took Liam. Your mom told them that Liam saved them from being beaten to death by going with the men. They were looking for something, and Liam told them he knew where to find it but insisted on showing them."

Feather has heard everything. She places a chair behind me just as my knees buckle. The boys become frightened, not knowing anything except my reaction as I speak on the phone. They try to grab the phone from my hands. I glare at them, telling them to shut up. The adrenaline of arguing with them helps to clear my head, and I answer James. "Eli and Fuller are with me. Can you tell me how long ago these men left with Liam? Was he all right when they left?"

"Here—you talk to the sheriff," James says. I hear him saying to someone that I'm on the phone, and then I hear the sheriff's voice.

"Coda, I'm sorry about what's happened, but everyone appears to be okay. Your sisters want to leave with my deputy and follow the ambulance. They say they'll call you from the hospital. Can you tell me what's going on?"

I look at Feather and she nods her head. She knows what this means when the law becomes involved.

"Sheriff, I need you to call the FBI for me, please. I can't give you the specifics, but I need help as well. Please find a safe number I can call to explain our situation," I say. My mind races to what we need to do—we have to leave this place immediately. We have to go to someplace to keep Feather safe, but I need to stay so I can help Liam when the men arrive with him. I know Liam will have figured out the clues left on the desk. He saved the folks. I'm so proud of him. I know he's not leading them to us of his own free will. He's being threatened, and this is the only way he saw to protect the family.

"Here's the number in Oklahoma City," the sheriff tells me. "It's 405-290—"

I interrupt. "Can you tell me the number for New Mexico?"

"Sure, just a minute . . . that number is out of Albuquerque," he says and then wishes us good luck.

I call the number, explain Feather's past, and what her father has done to my family. They transfer us to an agent, putting us on hold when they hear Feather's father's name. They say they've been tracking him ever since they found his wife murdered thirteen years ago. They knew the child was missing as well—she was never found but was assumed to be dead. Each time they get close to her father, he manages to slip away and then doesn't resurface for months. They can't prove it, but there are other unsolved missing persons who were involved with him. They say they'll make a plan and call back. Fuller has been watching the road and the cabins ever since we got on the phone, and now he sees Liam coming. Eli turns the Dodge around to face the gate so we can leave at the first sign of trouble. We figure Liam will come up with the same plan they did, and he will stop at the cabins.

"Feather, gather your things and whatever you think we might need. We're going to have to get you away from here if they come. We have to stay mobile until the FBI can help us, but we have to also stay close enough to help Liam," I say.

Several hours later, the phone rings; it's the agent. He says, "No one has ever reported a Falcon Feather or Charlotte Hilton missing or kidnapped. A woman identified as Feather's mother was found beaten to death, and the daughter was taken by the father years ago. Tell Feather that no charges will be filed against the grandfather, and she will not have to be with her dad. If we catch him, he will be behind bars and will never see the light of day again. We want to set a trap for him—a trap he can't get out of this time."

"They're here!" Fuller yells.

The agent hears him and gives me my instructions. "Have you been to Elizabethtown?"

"Yes," I reply, as everyone heads to the Dodge.

"Get them to follow you. Don't let them know you are aware of them. Drive straight to Elizabethtown. Go to the museum; it's off the highway and over a hill. We'll have everyone in place. We've removed the civilians, so anyone you see should be our men or women. Drive up to the old fire trucks on the hill and walk briskly down to the museum. Don't look around at Feather's dad; he mustn't suspect anything. Go inside, and one of our men will take it from there," the agent says.

"Got it. We're leaving now. Go to Elizabethtown, stop on the hill, walk to the museum," I repeat.

"Yes, good luck. Can you tell us what your brother looks like, maybe what he's wearing?" the agent asks.

"Do you see Liam? What is he wearing?" I call out to Fuller.

"His red Oklahoma University shirt and jeans. Why?" Fuller asks.

I relay the message and hang up. Feather and the boys are already in the Dodge. I'll fill them in on the plan as we go.

CHAPTER 16

LIAM, LIFE, & LOVE

I'm glad that Dad insisted we take the Dodge; it has four-wheel drive and where we're going, we may need it. I'm so glad there isn't snow down here in the valley. The roads are rough enough with rocks. We slip out of the gate and turn to drive by the cabins.

"I need you to tell me what these guys are doing, but don't be too obvious," I say.

"What are you doing?" Eli asks.

"We're going to get Liam's attention, if we can. They need to follow us, but we need to act like we don't see them or know them."

Fuller exclaims, "What? Are you crazy? They'll see Feather!"

"We have to get them to follow us. The FBI is setting a trap at Elizabethtown. We just have to lure them there. Feather, you and your grandfather will be okay. The authorities aren't after you, only your dad," I say, not wanting to tell her about her mother.

"I heard everything the man said on the phone. I know what happened to my mother," she says, watching the cabins. "There—they're coming out of the cabin's office. They're driving a blue two-door Malibu. They just shoved Liam in the backseat, and a man is getting in with him. The other two have split up, and one is looking toward the lake. The other is walking over to a cabin."

"Is it cabin number fourteen?" Eli asks, trying to see around Feather. "That's our cabin."

"Yes, he's at the cabin. He's looking around. He has a gun in the back band of his belt. He has it drawn . . . he's kicked the door in! The other is walking behind the cabins. I can't see him any longer," she says.

We drive by the cabins, heading north on Highway 64. As we pass, Liam is looking out the window of the Malibu and sees us. Fuller holds up a note to his window that reads: *Never fear. We are here. Follow us.* Liam's face is swollen, and he has a black eye, but he smiles. He turns to talk to his captor, who has been watching the cabins and didn't see us. We pull onto the highway at a normal speed. Feather and Eli face each other in the backseat, pretending to be talking to one another as they give us a blow-by-blow of what's happening.

"Liam must've told them that he saw us, because I hear a horn honking with one long blast. The other two are coming at a dead run," Eli says. "Step on it, bro. They see us and know what we're driving now."

I speed up but stay within the speed limit. The agent said they're ready, so I hope they know how close I am.

"Turn around. Let me watch them from the rearview mirrors. They can't know that we know they've seen us," I say.

Feather sits angled in the corner against the door and the back of the seat. Eli strikes the same position. They try to act like they are in a conversation with each other. Fuller keeps a constant watch on Liam and the men with the passenger's side mirror. I slow down, and they pull in behind me before we leave Eagle Nest. I think they're trying to decide the easiest way to take us. The highway is already very busy with traffic, so their chances of overcoming us without anyone seeing them are slim. I think they'll wait until we stop or until we are in a more isolated area.

"They're right behind us. Our plan is working perfectly," I say.

"Coda, you hardly have any gas!" Fuller exclaims.

I forgot that we'd come in so late, I'd decided to refuel this morning. How could I have been so stupid as to leave town without refueling?

"I'm afraid if we stop and get out, they'll approach us, and they could use Liam as a hostage to trade for Feather," I say, thinking out loud. "We have to keep moving. I'm sure I can make it to Elizabethtown. It's only ten miles."

We speed up to the maximum speed allowed, slowing down only as we approach the Elizabethtown turn-off.

"Well, here goes. We're here. I hope they're ready for us. Just in case, everybody find something to use as a weapon for self-defense. We have to drive all the way to the top of the hill. It ends in a dead end, the agent said. We're to pull up to a fire truck and walk down to the museum. I may try to angle the Dodge so that if they are close, we can exit from one side of the truck, using it as protection. No one turn around or look behind us; just walk briskly to the museum. What do you think?" I ask.

"I think we should exit from the driver's side. I can squeeze past the steering wheel faster than you can," Fuller suggests.

It's unanimous, and we all choose weapons—from a can of ether to a small pen knife.

"There's the fire truck! We're here—everybody ready?" Eli asks. "I don't see any vehicles. What if the law isn't here yet? What if we're too early? Everyone get ready to bail when we stop."

"No! Keep your heads and walk briskly to the museum, and don't look back. It is what they said to do," I say, trying to calm everyone.

As we pull up and stop, Feather and Fuller both ease toward the other side of the truck. I angle the Dodge. The way the old garage sits, it'll add some protection too. We're all looking at our surroundings, making plans if we have to run.

"There's a creek just ahead of us, and it looks like it skirts this small hill. If we run, let's head up that creek and separate after we have the cover of the trees. It'll be easier to double-back unseen and surprise them," I say, scanning the possibilities.

"I'll run straight up the mountain. They won't know where I'm going, but you will. They'll expect me to take an easy route, being a girl and all. But I'm in very good shape, and I've lived all of my life in the higher altitudes. I should be able to outpace them," Feather says with confidence.

The Malibu pulls into the drive where we are and stops. The men get out, and they're bringing Liam. I have my hand on the door handle and so does Eli. Fuller and Feather feel the tension and slide to the center of the truck. I wonder why the police aren't showing themselves. Then it dawns on me—the man walking with Liam has a gun pointed at Liam.

"The police are afraid to come out for fear of the men shooting Liam. Let's go. Fuller, you and Eli protect Feather. I'm cutting around behind them, using this garage to block their view. I've got to help Liam," I say. Before there is time for discussion, I yell, "Go!"

We bail from the truck and head to the museum. I slip unseen to the side of the garage. I run around the building, and I begin to think I've made a mistake. I round the corner, seeing Liam and his captor watching the pursuit as they stand in front of the Malibu. Liam's hands are tied behind his back. Everyone has made it to the museum and has disappeared from view by the time I make it up behind the captor. He turns around, and I take the tire iron that had been behind the seat and thump him on the head. He goes down. I grab his gun and untie Liam. A couple of officers come running up the drive to take the man into custody. The small town seems to come to life with people. Armed officers escort the other two men back to us. Finally, I see Eli, Feather, and Fuller emerge from behind the museum. My brothers are flanking her on either side, making sure big brother sees what a good job they are doing by protecting her.

"Wow, you chose to help me over protecting the girl?" Liam asks, grinning. "I must really rate after all."

I grab him and hug him, not caring who might see us. "I love you, Liam, and I don't want you to ever think that your life is unimportant to me," I say, with my voice full of emotion.

EPILOGUE

THE MISSION TRIP

"Are you sure it's all right with your mom that we leave the kids for a whole week?" Feather asks. "You know what a handful the twins can be since they started walking."

"I'm sure she is going to love every minute of it. God will provide what she needs. He'll soothe the twins, and God has already sent two grandfathers to help Mom with the kids. We'll be back before they know we're gone," I say as we load up the Jeep, preparing to head out to the remote Indian villages on the reservation.

When Feather and I married, we knew that our mission field would be right here in the United States. She is and has always been focused on telling every single person she knows about the Lord. My plan was to be a national forest ranger. I enjoy my job as a ranger, but it's these mission trips that give purpose to my life. I can't wait until the twins are older and they can go with us. From the moment I saw them in the hospital, those little girls had my heart, just as their mother did so many years ago. I'm so thankful they have their mother's firefly brown eyes. Fauna has dark brown hair, and her complexion is dark, like her mom's. Little Fawn has my strawberry blond hair, and her skin burns anytime she's in the sun, causing freckles to pop out across her nose.

As we pull to a stop at the reservation road, Feather says, "We forgot something, Messenger."

She knows how I love that name, and she always uses it affectionately. I ask, "What?"

"Let's pray," she says simply.

We bow our heads and pray that we might be used for the glory of God. We end with our favorite verse, Proverbs 16:9.

In his heart a man plans his course, but the LORD determines his steps.